The Boy on Platform One

BOOKS BY
VICTOR CANNING

The Boy on Platform One

VICTOR CANNING

HEINEMANN : LONDON

William Heinemann Ltd
10 Upper Grosvenor Street, London W1X 9PA

LONDON MELBOURNE TORONTO
JOHANNESBURG AUCKLAND

First published 1981
© Victor Canning 1981

SBN 434 10796 4

Printed and bound in Great Britain by
REDWOOD BURN LIMITED
Trowbridge, Wiltshire

Children pick up words
as pigeons peas, and
utter them again as God
shall please. Proverb

CHAPTER ONE

THE BOY ON Platform One at Paddington Station looked across its empty track to the high-speed train beginning to pull out from Platform Two. It was the train for Swindon, Bristol, Newport and Cardiff. Change at Swindon for Stroud, Gloucester and Cheltenham. In all his near fourteen years he had —except for a few visits to his grandparents in Ireland—never in his life been further west of London than Maidenhead, where his father had taken him once for a day on the river— though they had never got to board punt or skiff or to eat their sandwiches moored peacefully under some overhanging willow. It had rained all day and they had gone to the cinema and eaten in the back row of the stalls. There had been no disappointment in him. A day out with his father for company was a rare enough treat. And anyway, there was far more to see in London than in the country. Hyde Park—a few minutes' walk from his home—was good enough for him.

A station pigeon flew down to the platform a few feet from him. He pulled a hand from the slit pocket of his blue windbreaker and tossed it a small stale crumb of bread from the store which he usually carried with him. The bird had a ring on one leg and he knew that it must be an escapee from some loft ... may be far from London, somewhere in the country, far west or north. Some time or other the bird had come winging in and had decided to stay. Who wanted the country? London was where the action was.

He turned and wandered back to the main concourse and stopped at a confectionery booth. The middle-aged woman inside gave him a smile and said, "Hullo, Peter—you haven't got a spare pair of feet on you, have you? Mine are just about done."

He grinned. He liked May. He said, "I'm sorry, May. I just gave away my last pair to Blackie Timms. He said they were a bit tight but would do. He does a lot of walking, you know, sweeping up station rubbish."

"And I do a lot of standing. You put me on the list for your next pair, will you love?"

"Will do."

She put her hand into a sweet box and threw him a roll of mints which he caught. He put his fingers to his lips and blew her a kiss as he turned to walk away. He was an odd one, she thought. Not like some of the other scruffs who hung around the station. Here almost every Saturday. Always by himself. Yes, and definitely a cut above most of the others ... tell that, not by his clothes, windbreaker, jeans and sandals, but by his voice. Something of the gent there, and in a handful of years those blue eyes and that quick warm smile would turn some girl's heart over. Not to mention that tawny, russety brown hair that made you feel you wanted to stroke it ...

Peter usually left the station by going up the hotel steps and through the reception lounge and so out into Praed Street. Today the girl at the desk looked up and said, "Peter, you know you're not supposed to come through this way. The boss will skin you."

Peter grinned. "Not today he won't. Saturday. Arsenal are playing at home and he always goes to see them. Besides, how do you know, I might be coming to book a room?"

The girl laughed. "What for? Your honeymoon?"

"How'd you guess? I'm getting married next week."

"Who's the lucky girl?"

"Haven't made up my mind yet. Would you like to be put on the list?"

"No thanks. You're not my type. Now get moving."

"Okay."

As Peter went out of the main doorway into Praed Street, the clerk sitting behind her making ledger entries said, "Who is that kid?"

"Peter Courtney—he lives over Radnor Place way. Always here Saturdays."

2

"Pretty cocky and sure of himself, isn't he?"

"I suppose so, but in a nice way."

"When I was young we knew our place."

The receptionist sighed. "Yes, perhaps that was the big trouble. A new generation arises."

"So it does. One what wants its bottom kicked."

Peter walked along Praed Street, unmoved, almost unaware of its run-down sleeziness, its porn shops, steamy windowed coffee bars and its shabby mixture of broken down cultures. Since he was nine years old he had known this district and in four years he had become known and accepted though he had never become part of it. A coloured youth squatting in a doorway, sucking at a can of beer, grinned at him and said, "Hi, Pete. How things?"

"Hi, Fernie. Your old man out yet?"

"Next week. Gonna be a big party. You wanna come?"

"No thanks. But give him my best."

He moved on, then paused before turning into the newsagent's shop to get his father's evening paper. High against the darkening April sky an airliner drew a bright vapour trail. He watched the wind unravelling its sharp edges and wondered what it would be like, sitting up there, looking down. He had never flown in his life.

He went into the shop and picked up his father's *Evening Standard*, then fished in the back pocket of his jeans for the money to pay the monthly paper bill. He handed over the exact amount. His father always knew to a penny how much he owed.

The woman behind the counter, large and loosely aproned, gave him a smile and said, "You want a comic, Peter? Free on the house?"

He shook his head. "No thanks, Mrs H."

"Never read 'em?"

"Not really." It was almost a ritual exchange.

She smiled. "Never read?"

He grinned. "Only at school."

"It's all there, you know ... in books."

"I know ..." He paused, then smiled and said, "You've got

3

a new brooch on. I like it."

She laughed. "You don't miss much, do you? Seed pearls and a turquoise—or so my old man says which don't make it gospel. One of his horses came up for a change and he got drunk enough to be generous."

"I like Mr Harper."

She laughed. "So do I—some times more than others."

He turned away. When he reached the door, he paused and looked back over his shoulder and with a grin said, "But I like Mrs Harper better."

He went out, the sound of her laughter dying behind him. A little farther up the street he turned right and within a few hundred yards the dubious world of Praed Street was lost. A few minutes later he was in Radnor Place, the houses neat and well kept and withdrawn from the world behind white-curtained windows. Like most of the other houses the Court-ney house had a hanging basket over the front door and window boxes. In the hanging basket his stepmother had planted a maidenhair fern and a trailing geranium. The window boxes held stiff little formations of primula wanda, still tight-budded, and the paved narrow strip of front garden held two tubs planted each with a small bay tree. There had until recently been three tubs of bay trees but one had been stolen—a gardening hazard in these parts which the owners accepted—after a first outburst of violent language—philosophically.

Peter rang the door bell. Doors and windows were always kept locked. His stepmother, Joan, let him in. She was a neat, small, blonde woman in her late thirties, well-kept and a little vain of her looks. For the most part she was affable and easy-going, but when she lost her temper—which was seldom—it was with the suddenness and fiery display of a tropical storm. She was often alone for Peter during the week was at school and her husband Frank away at his antique and secondhand book shop in the Tottenham Court Road.

She gave Peter a kiss on the forehead and said, "Your supper's on the table in the kitchen. Then go up and change—I've put your clothes out. Your father will be here in about

4

three-quarters of an hour." She smiled. "So he said—but if we know him it'll be rush, rush, rush." She put a light hand on the back of his neck and ushered him down the hallway towards the kitchen. She had been married to his widowed father for three years and loved the boy but—without any great concern—still found herself at times wondering about the father. But then, she thought, as she began to busy herself in the kitchen, as the boy dutifully washed his hands under the sink tap, she had wondered about her first husband ... so perhaps that was the way it was with any man. You just went on wondering ... knowing that the best thing to do was not to let it get you down.

As she watched Peter eat—steak-and-kidney pie with a slip of bay leaf from one of the tubbed trees in the front of the house—she said, "I had a letter from your Uncle Chris today. He says he might be home soon. His ship's coming back for a refit or something. That please you?"

"Yes, it does. Where was he? When he wrote?"

"Oh, some foreign place ... in the Persian Gulf. Wherever that is."

Peter smiled, cleared his mouth of food and said, "If you really wanted to know I could show you in the atlas."

"Don't bother ... I'll get your sweet, but don't dawdle over it." She went to the refrigerator and brought out his plate of ice-cream and canned fruit.

While he ate she chattered away to him. Sometimes he listened and sometimes he just let her words wash over him. He liked her, but she had not in any deep way taken the place of his real mother. Sometimes, when he lay without sleep late at night, she would suddenly be there. Alive and clear in his mind, coming into his bedroom as though it were actually happening, and he could hear her say lightly, 'I knew you weren't asleep. Shall I tell you about the time the blackberry jam we were making at Granny's boiled over?' And there she would be, the little touch of her ancestral Irish in her voice, enchanting him with her story.

His stepmother said, "You like your Uncle Chris, don't you?"

5

"Yes. Lots."

"That's good then. He's a fine man."

As she began to clear the table and Peter stood up to go and change, she said from the kitchen sink, "Do you like doing what you do with your father?"

"I don't mind. He likes me to do it."

"Do you know how you do it?"

"No, I don't. It just happens. I think one day it'll go. Just like a boy at school who stuttered and then we were larking about and he fell and banged his head—and when he got up he didn't stutter any more."

She laughed. "You're making it up."

He laughed, too, and said, "Well, anyway, he didn't stutter anything like as bad as before."

Up in his bedroom he stripped to his underpants and put on the clothes his stepmother had laid out for him, his best navy-blue suit, a white shirt and a blue tie with a thin red stripe in it. In the pocket of his jacket was a small comb with which before he 'went on'—his father's phrase—he gave his hair a final tidy. Then he sat staring out of the window, waiting for his father, but thinking of his Uncle Chris who was his stepmother's brother. Somewhere right now he was at sea on an oil tanker. That was a funny life ... always moving about. Not his style, really. He liked to be where he belonged, where he knew the people and the places. Some of the boys at school were always talking of how when they left they would get out of the country ... go places. See the world ... But he liked to be in the places he knew and with the people he knew. What are you going to do when you grow up? People were always asking that question. Well, he didn't know. He was perfectly happy how he was and where he was. He supposed, though, in the end he'd go and help his father in the shop. Well, it wouldn't be so bad. Though it would be better if it weren't just old second-hand and antique books that he sold. Books. Some people were mad about them. His mother had been like that ... books ... poetry. Distantly in memory he could hear her voice now reciting poetry to him as he drifted into sleep. He went off into a reverie, thinking of his mother.

6

He came back to himself to hear his father calling from downstairs.

"Peter! Come on—we're late!"

* * * *

Sitting beside his father in the car as he drove down Hyde Park Street and turned left into Bayswater Road, Peter said, "Where are we going tonight?"

"Hampstead. It's a literary club."

"Oh . . ."

His father laughed. "You like men's clubs, don't you?"

"I don't mind. Not really."

"You wouldn't say if you did, would you? Anyway, it'll be an early night for you. You go on first and we do our bit. Then they have half their ordinary meeting and you come back and finish off, and then we're away. Feeling all right?" His father's left hand reached out and touched the side of his face briefly.

"Fine."

"Paddington today, as usual?"

"Yes."

"One of these days you'll get on one of those trains and be off like a bird. You want to watch it."

Peter laughed. But it was true, he thought. He liked men's clubs. They were jollier, and some of the stuff they gave him was really funny and sometimes a bit . . . well. His father didn't like it, but he didn't mind. He went off into a quiet mood. He liked the way his father drove. No fuss, and no losing his temper.

Frank Courtney knew the mood, sometimes felt that it was a form of preparation which the boy instinctively reached for, had to have, before he could perform. God knew . . . but whatever it was it worked and was a gift from the gods. There had been a time when he had worried about it for the boy's sake . . . wondering if there were harm in it for him . . . prepared to stop it if he made the slightest objection. But Peter never had and he had slowly come to recognize that the boy himself in some obscure way enjoyed himself. One day, perhaps, the gift would

7

go. In fact, he hoped it would. Boys should be normal. Not freaks. More than once he had made up his mind to stop it but something, perhaps sheer pride in his son, had made him keep on. You never looked a gift-horse from the gods in the mouth. There were dozens of things you should never do, but you found yourself doing them and then, looking back, wondered how in God's name you had ever started, ever made a trap for yourself.

If his first wife still lived she would never have allowed him to exploit it. All that had happened after she had died. As for Joan . . . well . . . she was too easy-going to have objections or even, he felt sometimes, much conscience about things as long as she was left comfortable and undisturbed in the dreamland she inhabited most of the day . . . the radio, the television, her women's magazines.

The house was a large one in an avenue off Haverstock Hill. He was lucky and quickly found a parking space. The club secretary met him at the door and he and Peter were ushered into a small side room.

The secretary said, "You're a little late, Mr Courtney. Everyone's waiting. Do you think you could go in right away?"

"Of course."

"I've explained the procedure to everyone." Then to Peter he said, "When you come out to wait in here there'll be some coffee and biscuits—or would you like a soft drink?"

"I don't want anything. Thank you very much."

The room was a large one with a small dais at one end on which were four chairs. There were between twenty and thirty people seated around the room. Peter looked at them without any particular interest as the secretary introduced them. He then sat down on one of the platform chairs as his father made his little speech before the proceedings began. He knew the speech by heart now and the one or two little jokes he made in its course. With these people the jokes were quite different from the ones he used in a men's social club—though those were mild enough compared with some the boys told at school.

"I have to say that the discovery of my son's gift was quite accidental. It was in fact discovered by my first wife. . . ."

8

So it was. Peter remembered it well. Every night after she had tucked him up in bed and he lay comfortable and warm, near ready for sleep, she would either tell him some story of her childhood in Galway, or perhaps read a piece of poetry to him. Not that he cared for the poetry much, but he liked her stories. Then one evening when she had come to the end of reading a poem, while he drowsed, feeling the comfortable cocoon of sleep thickening round him, she had said, "Peter—you've not been listening at all."

"Yes, I have, Mum."

"Then what was it?"

"What was what?"

"The poem I've just read."

"I don't know. How did it begin?"

Then in a slightly, but gently exasperated voice she had given him the first line—*I will arise and go now, and go to Innisfree* ... And from there he had taken up the lines and without any effort gone right through the poem, feeling in an odd way that it must be someone else speaking, to finish— *While I stand on the roadway, or on the pavements grey, I hear it in the deep heart's core.* He didn't know how he did it. Didn't really care much about it. He could just get comfortable and relaxed and let somebody read to him, the words washing over him, making no effort to give them importance or commit them to memory—and then an hour, a day, months later, if someone gave him the opening lines, the whole thing would come back to him. It was all daft really. In fact it made him feel a bit of a freak so that he never let on at school about it.

He sat now in front of all these people, his head bent forward, elbows on knees while the tips of his fingers just supported his bowed head which was the way his father preferred him to be. A little bit of stage business to give everyone the idea that he was going off into some other world when all the time he was just himself and still in a very real world and hearing his father say:

"I can offer no explanation for this remarkable faculty, and in no way do I intend to exploit it. But I feel it is quite proper in the right surroundings and with the right sort of people to demonstrate, as Shakespeare said—'There are more things in heaven and earth, Horatio . . .'"

His face hidden by his hands, Peter smiled to himself. His father used a quite different speech at men's clubs. He, himself, preferred them. They were much more fun.

" . . . I never allow more than four readings, verse or prose, in an evening. My son then goes away for an hour to be left alone in a room with someone, chosen from among yourselves, to see that there is no collusion or trickery involved. When he comes back the persons originally involved will in turn repeat the first line of their chosen pieces and my son will . . ."

Gabble it all off like a parrot . . . Peter smiled to himself. That's what his mother had said once. Poetry was meant to be spoken properly. But he couldn't help that. It had to come out just the way it did come out. But it hadn't often happened while she was alive. She wouldn't let his father cart him around much. Not like now, doing it sometimes three or four times a month. And, of course, his father got money for it, and why not? The old bookshop didn't do all that well and there were often rows between his father and his stepmother over her extravagance. She was always buying new clothes and going to the hairdresser. Though he couldn't see why not. She was very pretty and he liked the way her hair smelled when she came back from the beauty salon.

The first one to come up was a tall dark-haired lady, in a funny long, green dress and wearing open sandals over her bare feet. She was nice, though. And he liked the way she flickered her long eyelashes as he rose and shook her hand. She said in a warm voice, "Good evening, Peter." He said politely, "Good evening, ma'am." Then he sat down.

The woman announced, "I would like to read a poem of my own composing which was recently published in *Militant Verse*, and which I am quite sure will be completely incomprehensible to our young friend here and certainly not known to him."

Peter kept his face unmoved. It had happened before. They read their own work so that there was no hope that he could ever have known it.

"Are you ready, Peter?"

"Yes, ma'am."

He leaned forward elbows on his knees and covered his face with his hands. Not because it helped him to concentrate but he got embarrassed if he just had to stare at all the other faces watching him.

The woman began:

> Unmoved, unmoving, unmoveable
> Timeless, untimed, unloveable
> Forgotten, forgetting the days
> Paced by the slow cogs of time
> And the hour glass sand that spills
> No balm for our ills . . .

Frank Courtney suppressed a little sigh and breathed a gentle—*Christ*—to himself, and then to save himself from boredom fixed his eyes on a picture at the back of the room which showed a group of young, naked boys grouped on a sea rock, diving and swimming and lying out in the sun. It was a clear, bright, happy picture and the sharp thought suddenly took him that Peter should have been among them—out of this, out of London, in the country or by the sea. How often had Sarah said—"Why can't you take a country bookshop? Some place where we can breathe the good Lord's air, not man's stink." He went off into a guarded, watchful reverie until he heard the long-gowned poetess finish—

> No more the slow shuffle to
> The rejecting factory gate
> One step alone brings Time's release
> The portals ope
> To welcome living death to Eternal peace.

She finished to a tepid clapping of hands. Peter suppressed a sigh and straightening up, stood and held out his hand to her and said, "Thank you very much, ma'am."

"Thank you, Peter. I hope you liked it?"

11

Politely he said, "I think so, ma'am," and he grinned when everyone, including the poetess, laughed.

The chairman said, "And now may we have the second person please. Mr Rundell it is, I think. Is that right?"

Peter watched as a middle-aged, partly bald, thickset man, wearing a dove-grey suit and a canary-yellow waistcoat, rose from his chair and came forward and on to the low platform. Mr Rundell had a large, fleshy face, loosely dewlapped, which gave him the appearance of an amiable bloodhound. He came on to the platform, gave a little bow to the chairman and to his father, and then came to him and gently patted the top of his head and said, "Good evening, Peter."

"Good evening, sir."

Mr Rundell turned to his father and said, "Mr Courtney, I don't want in any way to embarrass you or your son, and I certainly wouldn't dream of pressing the point I am about to make. But I have a favour to ask you."

"Go ahead, Mr . . . ?"

"Rundell. Does your son learn French at school?"

"Yes, he does, but he's not very far advanced with it."

"Well, it occurred to me that the gift you claim for him must clearly be of a mechanistic order—linked far more to the sound of words than their meaning. Would you think so?"

"It could be, yes."

Peter knew his father's tone of voice and sensed that he distrusted the man. In a way it was the same tone old Blackie Martin at Paddington Station would have used if he thought anyone was being too clever with him. *Yuh tryin' to send me up, man?*

"Then I wonder if you would agree to my reading to Peter a French poem?"

Peter saw his father's face tighten in the lines of preliminary anger, the way it would at men's clubs sometimes when some man tried to go too near the knuckle with a ballad or bar-room ditty. Almost without knowing he was going to Peter heard himself say, "It's all right, father. I think I would like to try. It'll make a change from . . . well from . . ."

He had no need to say more for the room burst out laughing.

When the laughter died Peter looked across at his first customer and said, "I'm sorry, ma'am. I didn't mean—"

"I know you didn't, Peter." She gave him a warm smile and said, "But why don't you try it?"

He turned to his father and saw that the tight lines had gone from his face.

"I'm agreeable if you are, my son." Courtney turned to Mr Rundell. "He's never done anything like this before but if you wish to try ... well, very well."

Mr Rundell beamed. "That's very kind of you and very courageous of your son. Let's see what happens." As he spoke he pulled a small, limp-bound book from his pocket and opened it to a page marked by a folded piece of paper. With a smile at Peter, he said, "Would you like a few moments to compose yourself, Peter?"

"No, thank you, sir. I'm ready when you are." He leaned forward, elbows on knees and his hands over his eyes. French, he thought. *Je suis, tu es* and *où est la plume de ma tante?* Funny, no one had ever thought to do this before ... nice for his father if he didn't make a cow's mess of it, and one in the eye for Mr Rundell. Last term he had come three from bottom in French.

Mr Rundell began to read in a clear, well-modulated voice, a voice a bit like Monsieur Iffe his French master at school ... real froggy stuff.

> *Voici les lieux charmants, où mon âme ravie*
> *Passait à contempler Sylvie*
> *Ces tranquilles moments si doucement perdus....*

Listening, anxiety for his son's success natural in him, and also—if Peter should come out with flying colours—seeing a new dimension to this demonstrable faculty, he remembered how Sarah had once said that if God gave a person a rare gift it was common politeness to the Deity not to abuse it. God ... she had a way of talking that cut through to the bone of truth. Perhaps if he had found a country or seaside shop they would be there now and she with them. Though she had never said anything, he knew that London had imprisoned her and taken

13

her strength ... a simple cold, a rasping cough and within a fortnight she had gone from them. If she were here now there would never have been any of the underhand business going on in the Tottenham Court Road shop. It was nothing to scream about, but enough to have brought down an Irish whirlwind of protest on his head.

> *Que je l'aimais alors! Que je la trouvais belle!*
> *Mon cœur, vous soupirez au nom de l'infidèle:*
> *Avez-vous oublié que vous ne l'aimez plus?*

* * * *

Thinking it over now, Joan in bed with her radio playing, Peter deep in sleep in his room, and himself sitting down here in the drawing room with his nightcap of whisky before him, half-drunk, its ease in his blood relaxing him, he found himself unable to decide whether he was disappointed or pleased. When Mr Rundell had finished reading his poem—God knows what it all meant in French—Peter was led away to the small hall room, to rest there with one of the club's members to keep him company. Oh, people took nothing on trust these days. He could have gone to Peter with a hidden tape recorder—God knows what ploy, what device—that would have given the whole performance the stamp of truth. Sitting at the back of the room, he had listened to first one and then other members get up and read some composition, some verse, and then to the starling chatter of group criticism... *While I admire a certain mellifluosity in Mr Burton's word-patterns there is a distinct, and unpleasing distortion of the apposition of some rhythmic devices with the intended continuity of* ... Christ! These people were not even the kitchen sink of literature. Their works for the most part were the twice used tea-leaves of overwrought egotism and little talent. Not fit to spread around a rose bush to keep the summer soil humid. And then later—that bloody marvellous boy of his coming back, the ghost of his mother's face shining through his own as it always did when he was growing

14

tired. Sarah, my love, you should be living at this hour because for damned certain you would never have let it happen. Yes, my love. He walked in, as he walks everywhere, by himself and happy with it, and he trotted through unmoved, unmoving, all the forgotten, forgetting bloody days until the portals oped to welcome living death to Eternal praise. Yes, praise—they clapped their hands off, Sarah my love. And then Mr Rundell's French turn. Dislike it as you would have, you would have been unable not to feel proud. Peter just sat there, cool as a cucumber, and took his first line—and I was sweating for him. But he took his cue from Rundell and away he went. And I swear to God, my darling, that he not only had the man's words off perfectly, but there was more than something of the sound of the man's voice in his. Sarah, my love—what have we bred between us? I hope to God something with far more of you in him than of me.

He finished his whisky and breaking a self-made promise, as he did more often than not of an evening late, he got up and re-filled his glass generously, saying to himself, "What did we breed between us? I ask again, my love. No answer to that I know." And then, pleased—perhaps too pleased—Mr Rundell coming to him just before they left and saying, "Here's my card, Mr Courtney. Remarkable boy you have. Remarkable, but perhaps not unique. There have been others before him. Mozart composing at the age of four, Beethoven at eight, and Schubert at eleven . . . the human brain is still mostly undiscovered territory. I wonder if you would mind your son giving a private demonstration some time for a few carefully selected friends of mine. Not as a favour, of course. I can promise you a very healthy fee. You agree? Splendid. I'll be in touch with you before long."

He sat down at the table, cradling his whisky between both hands, staring at the card which lay on the table before him. E.C. Rundell, Esq., Flat One, Park View House, Bayswater Road, W 2 And very nice, too. No doubt, the top flat, and with a clear view across Hyde Park to the Serpentine and the full beauty of the setting sun to put a sparkle into the man's evening drink. And the memory was slowly rising in him that maybe he had seen the man before . . . perhaps once or twice in the shop, browsing through the books. With the memory came the thought that perhaps Mr Rundell was like some few others who used the shop, one of those—though perhaps of more affluent station—who walked delicately through mazes and caverns measureless to man down to a sunless sea that carried a variety of keels bearing the world's dark cargoes.

CHAPTER TWO

ERIC RUNDELL STOOD with his back to the room, looking
out of the window at the Thames. The tide had just turned
from its high and was running out now in a brown flood. Away
to his right on the other bank he could just catch a glimpse of
the long length of Westminster Bridge and the terraces of the
Houses of Parliament. A river police launch went upstream
slowly, breasting the tide, and a string of barges went down-
stream, a handful of gulls screaming and quarrelling over the
refuse and scraps from a gash bucket which a bargee had just
tipped over the side. Snappers up of unconsidered trifles...

Behind him Lord Endsworth said in his lazy, aristocratic
drawl, "Seems to have the hallmark of a bloody long shot if
you ask me. And using a snippet of a boy, too. Are you not, my
dear Rundell, being a little carried away by your love of the
bizarre?"

"I don't think so, Minister. Bizarre, yes. But it's hard solid
fact—and I'm convinced the boy could do it. It's the only way
we're going to get it. The Comte de Servais refuses to pass anything on paper or tape or to allow anyone to take a written
transcript of his words. I don't blame him. One slip-up and he
would be putting his own head on the block. And that's the
last thing naturally he wants or we for that matter. He could be
useful again in the future."

"You have faith in the boy?"

"So far, yes. But I want to arrange another demonstration
so that you can see and hear for yourself."

"See?"

"If you wish, Minister."

"No thank you, Rundell. You tape it and then I'll listen to

it. How long can he keep these things in his memory?"

"I don't know—but in a few days time I shall know. If you agree the French trip—they can be over and back in a few days. But, according to his father, whatever he memorizes just stays in his mind until he's given the opening key lines to release it. I gave him a far from easy piece by Nicolas Boileau-Despreaux."

"Who?"

"A French seventeenth-century poet."

The Minister pursed his big, fleshy lips, grunted, and said, "I don't know. Don't like it over much. Can't one of your regular people handle it?"

Rundell shook his head. "In this business there is no absolute trust. Whoever I sent might find that their name is on the list. Where would we be then?"

"God help us. What a world we live in."

"We have to do it in the way our French friend wants it. After he's done it he has to stay absolutely in the clear. And that's what we want too."

"What's the boy's father like?"

"Pleasant enough. But a sad sort of type. Second marriage. Not all that happy. And, anyway, he's already a little on the dark side of the moon. He runs this antique and secondhand bookshop in the Tottenham Court Road. It's all open and above board downstairs. But upstairs there's a private room for special customers—"

"Pornography?"

"No, nothing like that. It's a dropping and collecting place. A post office for all sorts. Lovers, business types, a few underworld people who like to keep their exchanges at arms' length, and, I suspect though he doesn't realize it, a few of our ilk from some of the London foreign embassies and so on."

"Has he ever been charged?"

"No. We and the police often find it's more helpful to let that kind of place run. Jump him on a small matter and you can say goodbye to landing a big fish one day. If you want a full dossier on him I can let you have it."

"No, thanks. So far as I am concerned he doesn't exist—and

this conversation has never taken place."

"I've your permission then to go ahead?"

Lord Endsworth laughed. "Your politeness touches me. If I said *No*—you'd still go ahead. You have, of course, some idea of what your French friend is anxious to get off his chest?"

"Vaguely, yes."

The Minister laughed. "A little flirting by la Belle France with, let us say, the Russian Bear?"

"I think this time something rather more than that. Shall I say, perhaps the names of some who have become the adopted children of the Bear?"

"Dear, oh dear. I wish I could be surprised. Anyway, go ahead."

"Thank you, Minister."

*   *   *   *

On a Sunday morning the ritual seldom changed. Peter and his father went to early mass, and then they drove to the shop, which was open until twelve o'clock for those customers who could not get away during the week. Peter spent the morning sweeping out the shop and the little office, dusting and tidying the books on the shelves in the lower room and, once a fortnight, cleaning the shop windows inside and out. It was a job he enjoyed because with the work was mixed a certain amount of friendly contact with the people who came into the shop, some of whom he had known long enough now almost to call friends. But the best part of the day came when the shop was closed and he went off to have lunch with his father in a small Italian restaurant in Charlotte Street. Afterwards they went to the Zoo, or the Tower of London, or perhaps took a pleasure boat from Westminster Bridge and went down river to Greenwich. This was a day when they were together, not talking a lot, but happy in one another's company. The time had been when his mother had always been with them ... and it often seemed to him at odd moments, when some sight or sound flicked his memory, that she still was and he felt a swift touch of loss ... and sometimes he felt it happened to his father as

19

well. He would go silent for a long while and then, suddenly, as though shaking himself free from some dream or memory, would come back to earth and start telling his funny stories.

Sunday, too, was a pleasant day for Joan Courtney. With both her men out of the house until God knew what hour she was free to laze and slop about the house just as she wished. Not that she was any slattern. She kept herself and her house neat and tidy, but it was pleasant to slop around during the morning in her dressing gown, to smoke and drink coffee in the empty house and read the *Sunday Express* and the *News of the World* without distraction and, as the kitchen clock struck twelve, to pour the first of the few sherries she enjoyed before making a cold lunch for herself.

This morning, just as the clock struck twelve and her hand was going out for the sherry decanter, the telephone rang. When she picked it up she recognized the voice at the other end at once.

"Chris!"

"Joan—surprised?"

"I'll say I am. Where are you?"

"London. Flew in this morning."

"But I thought you were—"

"In the Gulf? No. Head Office called for me. I think it means promotion and a new berth. I've just booked in at the Strand Palace Hotel. I get an early train to go North tomorrow. No point in bothering you for a night except ... well, why don't you come along and have some lunch and a chat? Where are the other two? Off on their usual Sunday jaunt?"

"Yes. You know them. Regular as clockwork."

"How's the boy?"

"Fine."

"And Himself?"

"Just the same. Oh, Chris—I wish you'd given me some warning. My hair's—"

"Your hair's fine. It always is. Now get your skates on. I'll be waiting in the foyer. See you."

Ten minutes later, a little breathless from her quick changing, she left the house and caught a taxi.

At that moment Peter and his father sat contentedly at their lunch table, their two plates liberally loaded with *spaghetti bolognese* and a small carafe of red Chianti between them.

Frank Courtney smiled to himself as he watched his son tucking into his food. The boy, as all boys should have, had a good appetite and few fads. A boy without appetite, his Sarah had always said, must have some immortal sin on his soul or a real bad stomach ulcer.

He said, "What do you want to do after we've eaten?"

"I dunno, Dad."

"Well, do you think you could make a little mental effort and find out? My aim is to please—so long as it doesn't make a big dent in my pocket book."

"What did you do with your Dad on Sunday afternoons?"

"Depended on the time of the year. Summer we'd either go to a cricket match or swimming in the river. Winter we'd go to a football match or a long walk over the downs, all wrapped up—and then home to tea and toast with strawberry jam. That's where I first met your mother. Up on the downs with her father—both over from Ireland on a visit to relations. You wouldn't believe it—you could see in all directions for twenty miles. Everything laid out like a large scale map below them and there they were—lost. They had the happy knack of easily losing themselves and not caring much."

"She wasn't very old then, was she?"

"Nor was I—fifteen."

And, he thought, never another serious glance at a woman for the rest of their time together. First letters, then an exchange of visits either way, and then she had come to London to go to art school. After four years, when she realized with her down-to-earth good sense that she was never going to be another Dame Laura Knight or Anna Zinkeisen she had become an assistant in a West End store and they had finally married. And then after her death, although there was not another woman on earth like her for him, but he had the boy and it was better to marry than to burn, he had married once more—and as far as it went he had no real grumbles.

Peter said suddenly, "I'd like to go out to Heathrow and watch the aircraft."

"O.K.; will do."

He took the wine carafe, topped up his glass, and then offered it to Peter, who shook his head.

"Don't you like wine?"

"It's all right. If I put water in it."

Courtney smiled to himself and then said, "By the way, you know that Mr Rundell who gave you the French poem to remember?"

"Yes."

"He wants you to go and do your bit for him and some friends at his flat. Would you like that?"

"You want me to?"

"Only if you don't mind. Didn't you like him?"

"Oh, yes—but not as much as the lady in the funny long dress though. She had painted toe nails, you know. Green."

"Didn't you like that?"

"I didn't mind . . ."

I didn't mind. I don't mind. Always there was something in the way he spoke the words that unsettled him almost to the point of inexplicable guilt.

An hour later they were at Heathrow watching the movement of aircraft, the boy with his elbows resting on the balcony rail, his chin cupped in his winged hands and, he felt, not deeply interested in all that was going on. These were the times when his own loneliness stirred inside him, cold and coiling. What was there about trains and Paddington which brought the boy to life? He had gone to the station once to meet him and had watched him unawares for a while and seen a different person, known, liked, cheeky, laughing—a boy he seldom saw at home. God knows he had done all he could, loved him because he was of her flesh and his, and had married again solely to bring another woman into their lives . . . to give him what every boy should have. So far as it went it was all right. But it did not go far. Joan did her best—and sometimes it was better than his. No, perhaps often better. But she lived in some dream world of her own . . . the world of her magazines, recipes and beauty hints, profiles of the famous, home decorating and the mildly salacious undertones of answers to correspondents on the Problem Page to undercut the euphoria of their sentimental love stories.

At that moment in a bedroom at the Strand Palace Hotel, the noise of traffic coming muted through the closed windows, Joan Courtney and Christopher Lang lay in bed with one another.

Joan, her face a little puffed from love-making, lay on her back and stared at the ceiling where now and again the flash of reflections from the sun on car windows outside winged across the plaster like strange, misshapen birds. After a while she sighed and said, "I don't like it, Chris."

Lying on his back, his eyes closed, his hands clasped behind his head, the sun and wind-browned arms dark against the pale blue of the pillows, Chris sighed and said sleepily, "Oh, no—not that again Joanny..."

"Yes, that again. We ought to be honest and straighten the whole thing up."

"No dice. It would hit the poor bugger like an earthquake. And what about the boy? Couldn't do that to the lad, either. He'd come to know. What's wrong with this? It doesn't happen very often and it suits us both. You made a mistake and I made a mistake. This is the cosy answer to it. I'm not going to upset any apple-cart."

"What about your conscience?"

"Oh, that ... well, it nags sometimes, but not that often. Anyway, it damned nearly could have been the truth. You were as good as widow for a year nearly before I turned up again. The firm wrote me off. Everybody. Far as he was concerned, when I came back and found you married again, I think it showed good sense to let things be. You never were happy about me being away so long at a time." He laughed. "You lost a husband and you gained a brother. All neat and tidy—and I'm not the jealous type. You know that."

"All I know is, you could have come back much earlier if you'd wanted."

"I wanted time to sort things out—and that's just what we

23

have done. It suits everyone. Even those that don't know about it. I'll bet you he goes around dreaming about his first wife all the time. As for the boy—well, who says I'm not a good uncle to him? And I like him. We get on fine. Although some don't know about it—it suits everybody."

"Not me . . ." Joan sighed. "Sometimes I think . . ."

"Think what?"

"Well, God knows about it."

"For Pete's sake. Look—" he rolled on to his side and pulled her towards him, "—I promise you I'll never make any trouble. I'm away for months on end. When I come back I'm your brother. Long may it last. If you loved him, really went for him, I'd cast off and be away for good. But you don't. And don't bring up the God business. He's got enough on his plate without bothering about us."

She turned her face from him as he went to kiss her. "Well, I suppose so, but I just wish . . . well, that I wasn't such a stupid sort of woman. When I was a girl I had all these lovely dreams and thoughts—and I was good. No man but you ever touched me until I was married. . . ."

"Listen. . . ." he sighed. "There's nothing to worry about. Life deals you your hand of cards and, long or short with trumps, you got to play them the best you can. Now come on. The moment you say *finish* that's it. But until then, all we have to do is to be careful and enjoy ourselves."

*   *   *   *

From the window of Mr Rundell's study on the top floor of the block of flats there was a fine view of the park. The light was beginning to go fast and the street lamps were already on. Peter shrugged his shoulders a little to ease the fit of his best suit and ran a finger around the edge of the stiff collar his father had made him wear. When we do our best we must look our best, his father had said. Which wasn't like him. As long as he looked tidy his father usually never bothered what he wore so long as he was comfortable.

"It's a lovely view, isn't it, Peter?"

"Yes, ma'am." He turned and gave her a smile. She had come to stay with him after he had done the first part of his demonstration. He liked her. He didn't know why. Just liked her the same way as he liked May at Paddington. But she was very different from May—tall, and very dark-haired, elegant in a simple black dress and wore nice chunky bracelets and things on her right wrist. She smelled nice, too. Miss Lloyd was her name and she was looking after him here while his father talked in the large lounge with the men there.

She said, "You don't live far away, do you? Do you often go into the Park to play?"

"No, ma'am."

"Where do you like going?" She came close to him and—just as his stepmother did sometimes—she put both hands to his tie knot and straightened it a little. He didn't mind. With some people you were right away easy. With others, men and women, there were those who gave you a funny feeling. You knew you were never going to be quite right with them. With his Uncle Chris it was a bit like that—and with Mr Rundell.

"Paddington Station," he said. He expected her to give a little laugh. Most people did, as though he had said something very odd. But she said quite naturally, "That's very interesting. When I was a girl I was mad about Kew Bridge ... any bridge really. I just liked to look over and watch the water. Sometimes spit in it. Water flowing is the one thing I can watch for ever."

He laughed. "Something like that with me, too. I like to see the trains going out and all the people, sitting there like a ... well, like a film going by you and I wonder where they're all going. But I like the people on the station, too. The ones that work there ... they don't care anything about the people, you know. I said to Blackie Timms one day—he's a cleaner-upper, you know—did he like being with people all around all day."

"And what did he say?"

He laughed. "He said—'What people? I only see feets and litter, boy.' And the woman what keeps ... who, I mean, keeps the sweet kiosk was the same. You know what she said people were?"

"No."

He laughed and looking into her face saw that her eyes were dark, dark brown like polished chestnut conkers, and then he said, "She just gave a grunt and said like Blackie, 'What people? All I ever see is Mars Bars, Maltesers and so on and sometimes a *Hey, missus, this ain't the right change.*'"

Miss Lloyd laughed. "And what do you see when you look at people?"

"Not much really when I see them. But sometimes, long afterwards, they come back to me. It's funny that, really. Just lying on my bed reading and suddenly someone comes back to me and then I see everything."

"Right down to the last button?"

"Well, almost."

"Is that how your memory for words comes back to you?"

"I don't think so. I don't really know anything about that. It just happens."

"It must be useful at school—being able to remember like that."

"Oh, no! I don't do it there. I can't. I don't know why, but I can't. I have to do it ... well, like for someone else. Like my Dad. And I'm glad I can't do it there. People would think I'm a freak or something. That would be awful!"

She laughed again and put out a hand and just touched him on the cheek with the line of her knuckles. At that moment the study door opened and Mr Rundell came in. He was wearing a green smoking-jacket and tartan trousers and holding a cigar, the aroma from it moving to Peter and making him sniff a little.

Mr Rundell said, "Well, I think we can go on with the second part now. Have you two been having a nice chat?"

"Yes, thank you, sir."

With Peter sandwiched between Miss Lloyd and Mr Rundell they went back into the large lounge. The lights were on now and the curtains drawn across the wide stretch of windows. The room was a little hazy with smoke. Six people, all men, including his father, were ranged about the room in easy chairs and on a long divan, most of them had glasses at

26

their sides and two were smoking cigars. Peter caught his father's eyes and smiled. He knew that—no matter how often they did this—his father always had a touch of the jitters before he began. Only three of the people had given him a reading ... two of them in verse and one in prose. Peter sat down in a small armchair to one side of the large fireplace in which he had originally sat during the first session. He liked the fireplace. It was of white marble, the long length of the mantel shelf supported at each end respectively by a merman and a mermaid. The mermaid's face reminded him vaguely of his stepmother, smooth and fixed and unwrinkled. She didn't look very interesting. The merman, however, was, except for colour, old Blackie Timms to a T—lined and soured.

Before anyone could speak Peter said to Mr Rundell, "Please, sir—can I have a few moments to compose myself?" He didn't usually ask for this, or need it, but his father had suggested it. *Just a touch of showmanship, old son. They go for it, you know.*

"Of course, Peter. Take your time, and say when you're ready."

Peter leaned forward and rested his forehead on the tips of his spread fingers. Showmanship, he thought. And why was his father so anxious about this demonstration? He could always tell. Smoke, smoke, smoking away at cigarettes and all over him—well, he didn't mind—but you could have too much. Perhaps Mr Rundell was a big customer at the shop. But he doubted it. They didn't have any big customers. Some rummy ones, though. Particularly some of the ones that used the upstairs private book room. Rummy too—there was one man here tonight that he thought he had seen a couple of times about a month ago on a Sunday morning. He'd given him some verse, too, this evening. Miss Lloyd was nice. She understood about Paddington and people and on her gold bracelet one of the little, dangling charms was a locomotive. Perhaps she was a secret train lover....

After a decent interval—not too short, not too long, as his father had always said—he straightened up and said, "I'm ready, sir."

27

"Very good, Peter. Now let's have the first quotation. Jimmy, I think it was you. And remember—just the first line."

Keeping his head a little bowed still, hardly looking at the first man who had risen, book in hand, Peter let the first line wash over him. . . . *Ere on my bed my limbs I lay, God grant me grace my prayers to say:*

The man stopped reading and Peter took up the lines '*O God! preserve my mother dear—In strength and health for many a year . . .*' and then went through to the end of the poem . . . '*That after my great sleep I may—Awake to thy eternal day! Amen.*'

There was a pleasing round of applause as he finished. And he liked that—the applause. Always did. Even though it wasn't anything really, not really, to do with him.

The next man was very fat and very jolly looking with a monocle in his eye and a big cigar held between two fingers as he read from a book of verse—*The night it was horrible dark—the measles broke out in the Ark.*

Peter took it up easily, grinning broadly, '*Little Japhet, and Shem, and all the young Hams, Were screaming at once for potatoes and clams*'—and went on to finish to a gentle round of applause.

The last man was in his middle-thirties, tall, thin and dark-jowled, with long black hair flopping over one eye and, as he read his opening lines, there was a flash of gold tooth in his mouth.

The man read: '*They pulled the boat well above the tide mark and to make it safe he tied the long bow rope to a heavy boulder*'.

Peter smiled to himself. He had liked this bit. He went on— '*Then wearing his sword and carrying his spear he sent the dogs ahead . . .*' As he went on he wondered what the book was because he felt he would like to read it. He finished: '*Just below the sky-line stood a group of round, stone-walled huts, roofed with weather-browned turves.*'

There was a round of applause. He liked that. Then Mr Rundell came to him and patted him on the shoulder and said, "You are a remarkable young man. Remarkable. But now Peter—and this is with your father's permission—I would like Miss Lloyd to read you something and to see if you can go on with it. You like Miss Lloyd, don't you?"

28

"Yes, sir. I think she's super."

There was laughter all round and Mr Rundell said gallantly, "And so do we all. Would you like to have a try? There's no trick to it. But I don't want to say any more than that."

Out of the corner of his eye Peter caught his father looking at him, and then give him a little nod of his head. He said, "I'll have a try, sir."

"Thank you, Peter. Now when you are ready just say so."

Peter leaned forward with his elbows on his knees and shut his eyes, not because it helped but because he knew it would be what his father would like him to do. After a moment or two, he said, "I'm ready, sir."

From away to his left Miss Lloyd began to read—

> *Voici les lieux charmants, où mon âme ravie*
> *Passâit à contempler Sylvie*
> *Ces tranquilles moments si doucement perdus . . .*

When she stopped, without any feeling of surprise or triumph and not really caring, except for his father's sake, Peter took up the lines which he had first heard at Hampstead nearly two weeks before and went through them without a stumble, word perfect to the end—*Avez-vous oublié que vous ne l'aimez plus?*

Everyone clapped and Miss Lloyd came to him and for a moment he was afraid she was going to kiss him. But she put her hands on his shoulders and gave him an affectionate little shake.

"Peter, you're marvellous. Marvellous!"

He didn't think so, but he gave a little smile and said, "Oh, I don't know." And the willowy young man with floppy black hair and a gold tooth came up to him and said, "Well done, youngster. First class. Are you good at French at school?"

"Not very, sir."

"Nor was I once. Où est la plume de ma tante, eh? Why is it French tantes are always losing their blooming plumes—must be a moulting old lot, eh?" He laughed, delighted with his own joke, and Peter laughed with him, too, because he didn't think it was too bad either.

And then his father was at his side, happy and glad for him—and proud, too, Peter knew. Well, that was all right. He liked to see him happy and enjoying himself. Then his father said, "I've got to stop and talk a little business with Mr Rundell. I shan't be long but Miss Lloyd has her car here and she's said that she will run you home. Tell Joannie I shan't be long. That all right?"

"Of course, dad."

It was funny, he thought, that he very seldom said—*Your mother*. Not when he meant Joan. However, it was not a thought which lived long in his mind. Miss Lloyd took him home—but not directly. She had a cream-coloured Mercedes two seater and, as the Park was still open, she took him for a drive through it first, and just now and again for his pleasure she ignored the speed limit and zipped it up above sixty.

"You'll get caught," he said laughing.

"Then do you know what I would do?"

"No."

"Just waggle my eye-lashes at the officer and say I'm sorry. And do you know what he would do?"

Peter laughed. "Course. He'd say—Don't try that one, lady."

"Sadly, yes."

After a while Peter asked, "Were all those people there tonight friends of yours?"

"Oh, yes. All old friends."

"The one with a gold tooth and floppy hair—I liked him, he made me laugh."

"That was Teddy Tampion. He's great fun. Always full of jokes. He works with Mr Rundell."

When she dropped him at his home, she leaned forward and gave him a good-night kiss, and then watched him until he went into the house.

As she drove away she felt a rare mood of self-dissatisfaction begin to mount in her. God in heaven, she thought—the things we do.

*　　*　　*　　*

The two of them were alone now; Mr Rundell in an arm-chair, a balloon glass of brandy on the octagonal, pie-crust table at his side, a cigar, seldom drawn on, sending up a slow smoke signal, in one hand. Beside his own chair was a low glass-topped table, the glass chased with a design of the goddess Minerva, and on it a silver tray which held a decanter of whisky and a soda siphon and, now and again, his own glass when he put it down to light a cigarette. The silver ashtray, for convenience, he had balanced on the arm of the chair which was deep and made it awkward for him to sit up straight. Not that he wanted to sit up. He felt drained and suddenly tired, not physically, but emotionally . . . knowing somewhere in his bones, and in the remembrance of half-forgotten dreams, perhaps, that this was the day and the hour which had always been waiting for him. Oh, yes, all very civilized, and very few things positively stated by Rundell—except that he had quite a high position in the Foreign Office.

"All you have to do is as I have stated, Mr Courtney. You go to France with the boy—two or three days at the most—and you'll have Miss Lloyd to handle all the details." Rundell gave a little laugh. "A jolly trip. Pleasant company. You'll meet someone who will read to the boy. Nothing offensive, of course. By the way—how good is your French?"

For a moment a spark of resentment glowed in him. "Lousy. I'm sure, though—you must have checked that," he said.

"Naturally. As we have a few other things. For instance your top room at the shop. We could make trouble there, as you must guess. But—" he laughed briefly "—I don't think we need go into anything like that. You do this and you will be handsomely paid and you will be left alone. We're not recruiting. This is a once and for all . . . well, shall we say, favour that we ask of you?"

"And of Peter?"

"Good God—of course! Yes, of course. This just happens to be an occasion when our French client, shall we say, refuses to put anything in writing or to pass any form of document. He will just quote a short piece to the boy. But I don't attempt to deceive you—what he will quote is of very much importance. But only to us."

"And what do I tell my wife?"

"I don't think you want any advice from me on that score, do you? I understand that she is not of a very enquiring type of mind."

"You people do your homework, don't you?"

Rundell shrugged his shoulders. "Attention to detail. No success or survival in any walk of life without it."

Frank Courtney was silent for a while and then, almost as though he were hearing some other man speak, some alter ego surfacing and taking over, he said, "How much?"

Rundell picked up his glass. He swirled the brandy in it gently, then raised it to his nose and took the bouquet but then put the glass down without drinking.

"There would be two payments. One for you and one for your son. After all he is the one who figures principally in this. For you—two thousands pounds on your return from France. For your son—two thousand pounds to be put in trust and which nobody but he can touch, and not he until he is twenty-one. I apologize for the age of twenty-one instead of the present majority of eighteen. But in our business we are still a little old-fashioned about some things."

"And what danger is there?"

"None, I assure you. Just a trip to France. A private session such as tonight—but with only one man to give a reading. And that's it. You come back and the boy gives a repeat of what has been said to him and then you are both free, absolved, forgotten. Oh, yes—and nobody will ever bother you at your bookshop. Nobody. When we give our word—we don't break it. Please, do help yourself to more whisky."

He helped himself to whisky, silent, thinking, knowing he was being tempted, not under-estimating the power of the temptation, and—suddenly—wondering what the hell Sarah would have said could she have known these moments? And then not wondering. Her answer would have been straight and probably coarse for she had a rich Irish directness of speech when roused.

He said, "Can I think it over and let you know?"

Rundell shook his head. "I'm afraid not. Time is running short and there are things to be arranged which will take a little while."

"And if I say no?"

Rundell smiled. "We don't run an inquisition. You are a free man. You can say no—and walk out of here. And we would pass nothing to the police about your shop. But one day, in the nature of things, you would come a cropper. Your boy would know about it... Oh, come Mr Courtney, see sense. Perhaps to help you I will be indiscreet enough to say that what we want done is for this country's good. But I'm sure you don't want me to start singing a patriotic song."

Courtney stood up, glass in hand, and walked away from the fireplace to the far side of the room. On the wall directly in front of him was a framed photograph of an Oxford college eight. His eyes ran over the list of names underneath and found that of Rundell. E.C. Rundell. With a sardonic lift of humour in him he thought ... E.C. No doubt of what his school and college nickname would have been. Easy Rundell. But not now.

He turned suddenly, spilling a little of his whisky, and said harshly, "All right. We'll do it."

*　　　*　　　*　　　*

He came in just after the clock in the hall had struck eleven. Distantly she heard him move about the kitchen ... probably making himself a cup of instant coffee. That meant he had probably had a few drinks. Not that he was a heavy drinker. Only now and again when some mood took him he might go over the limit and then, when he came up, he would go and sleep in the spare bedroom which Chris used when he stayed with them. He was kind and considerate, but not over-loving. Though he had been in the early days. Both of them a little mad really. She, because of Chris's death ... so say! The bastard! And he, because the loss of the other one was fresh in

33

his mind and his heart. The Irish witch. She'd called her that in one of their infrequent quarrels. However, she'd married him in good faith and when Chris had turned up again she'd been talked into the brother arrangement which Chris had suggested—because it suited him fine—and to which she had agreed largely because of all the upset it would mean. And the boy to be considered, too. Kids didn't ought to have their lives mucked about. They liked things around them to be solid and stable.

She heard him come upstairs and go to the bathroom and then after a while the sound of his movement down the landing to the boy's room. No night did he ever miss that. If the boy was awake she would hear the sound of their talking for a while, and sometimes a sleepy laugh from the boy. He was a great one for joking, particularly if he'd had a few drinks. There was no talk or laughter. The boy was miles away in the land of Nod. He'd looked flushed and a bit excited when he had come back. Full of talk of the woman who had driven him home.

He came into the room, closed the door quietly and then said softly, "You awake?"

"Yes."

"Sorry to be late."

"S'alright. Did everything go well?"

"Yes."

He came over to her, a darkness above her against the pale light of a street lamp filtering through a gap in the badly drawn curtains.

"He seemed tired when he came in."

"He was bloody marvellous." He sighed. "Sometimes I think I ought to stop it all. Never should have started. Something seems wrong about it..."

She was silent for a while. She could easily start something by saying the wrong word. Sometimes she deliberately did that. When things were bad between them. But not tonight, when the badness was all on her side.

She put out a hand and touched him, saying, "Would you like to come in for a cuddle and a warm up?"

34

He sat on the edge of the bed, leaned forward and kissed her, and said, "Not tonight, thanks love. I'm bushed."

"Peter looked overdone. All flushed up and full of talk. You sure all that stuff is good for him?"

"I don't know. Perhaps not. But he seems to enjoy it. I was thinking . . ."

"Yes."

"There's a customer . . . wants me to go over to France soon to value some books . . . rare stuff he's got his eye on. Just for a few days. I thought I'd take Peter along. Make a change. He'd like it, I know."

"What about his school?"

He gave a short grunt. "To hell with them. Travel broadens the mind . . ."

"And the shop?"

"No problem there. Jensen can run it with one hand. He won't mind coming full time." He laughed. "Glad to get away from that witch of a sister he lives with. Anyway . . . we'll see."

He touched her cheek with the back of his hand and stood up. As he moved towards his bed she said, guilt turning slowly in her, "Sleep well, my love."

"And you."

CHAPTER THREE

THE WHOLE THING, he thought, was a bit of a lark. Fun.
Though—when he got back—nothing much to boast about to
the other boys. Most of them had been abroad. All over the
place with their parents. Though, he supposed, you could
count Ireland where they had gone often to visit his mother's
people. They were all right too. His grandfather Patrick had
taken him fishing once on a lough where he had been as sick as
a dog and then got a hook in his finger and the local doctor had
had to cut it out and give him injections ... *just to stop you
foamin' at the mouth and runnin' round biting people, though the good
Lord knows there's a many in this place could do with it to liven them
up* ...

He wore his jeans and a new windbreaker for travelling, but
in his father's suitcase was his best suit in case—as his stepmother had said—he went into company. Though he couldn't
see what company since his father was just going over to value
some old books for a Frenchy chap who lived in a château
place somewhere on the River Loire. Which he knew about, of
course, because it was one of the big rivers of France and it
came into one of the Captain Hornblower books when he
escaped down the river from a froggy prison, or something like
that. And his father saying he would fix it all up at the school
when they got back. What was nice, too, was that his father
had got this job through Miss Lloyd because the man they
were going to see was a friend of hers and she was going to
meet them in France and drive them down to the château.
Only thing was, he hoped he wouldn't have to speak much
French because he wasn't very good at it. *Où est* the *plume de ma*
bloomin' *tante?* That was the tall drawling man at Mr

Rundell's. Mr Tampion—the one with the gold tooth and the floppy black hair.

They went by train to Southampton and got on the ferry for Cherbourg, and he took the pills his stepmother had given him for seasickness. Though his father said that pills didn't really do anything. It was all in the mind. According to how your tummy was built you either would or wouldn't be. Luckily his tummy was the right kind.

They stayed the night in a small hotel in Cherbourg and he had the biggest prawns he'd ever seen in his life, plaice and chips, and an enormous slice of cake with ice-cream. He lay in bed without sleep, listening to the traffic noises outside and thought how nice it would be to see Miss Lloyd again, and how he was enjoying himself. Still, nice though the cross-Channel boat had been, it didn't really compare with a train, not one of the high-speed jobs that went like a great yellow-and-blue snake, slow at first and then—whoosh!

His father came up to bed, early for him, and they lay for a while in the dark talking. That was something new. Just being together, the two of them, in one room.

Before he was getting really sleepy, his father said, "This man Miss Lloyd is taking us to—he's heard about the way you remember things. From her, of course. If he asks you to do it for him—would you mind?"

"Not if she wants me to."

"It'll be in French. But not very long."

"French or not—it's all the same, isn't it? Just words. That's all it is to me. Just words ... well, not even that really. Just a lot of sounds. Like music. Do you think when we get back Miss Lloyd will come and see us sometimes?"

"I wouldn't be surprised. Did I tell you Uncle Chris is back in England?"

"No. Why hasn't he been to see us?"

"He's in Glasgow with his company. He thinks he's going to have to take over a new ship. He'll be down to see us some time. He telephoned your mother."

"Oh, good ..." He yawned. "You know I think I could get to really like ships ... yes, I think I could, but not as much as . . ." His voice died away in a mumble as sleep took him.

The next morning they had breakfast in their room. If you could call it breakfast, Peter thought. Just a big bowl of coffee and some curled around pastry things that exploded all over the place when he tried to spread butter and apricot jam over them.

Soon after breakfast, when they were all packed, Miss Lloyd called for them. When she gave Peter a big hug and a kiss on the cheek he didn't mind all that much, but he was a bit disappointed that she hadn't got the Mercedes. Instead there was a big Renault 16 with a left-hand drive. Anyway he soon forgot about the Mercedes because she told him to sit alongside her while his father went into the back and she gave him the map to follow the route to the place they were going to which was called Angers, but it was soon pretty clear to him that she didn't need any help from the map because she knew the way already. And it was funny, too, that she acted a bit differently with him now that his father was with them. Nice—but not so . . . well, easy. Anyway, he enjoyed following the way on the map. Down the Cherbourg Peninsula to Avranches, across to Laval through Fougères and then on to Angers. On the way they stopped for a picnic lunch she had brought and ate it on the banks of a river near a place called Château Gontier. The river was called the Mayenne and ran all the way down to Angers and finally joined up with the Loire. In a way, he thought, it was like having a geography lesson—but far more fun. After lunch he wandered away up the river to find a place to do a jimmy-riddle. On the way he passed a man fishing and, suddenly daring because he really was enjoying himself, he said after a little thought, "Bonjoy, monsieur. Avez-vous . . . uh . . . uh . . . caught quelquechose?"

The man turned, gave him a grin and said, "No, I bloody haven't, son. And by the look of things I don't bloody well expect to. Where you from?"

"London."

"So am I. Belsize Park. Wish I was back there, but the wife's gone all continental and French cathedrals. Never marry a woman what goes for culture and self-bloody-improvement, lad. They can never keep it to themselves.''

While he was gone Miss Lloyd said to Frank Courtney, "You're booked in at the Hôtel Champagne, that's quite near the Gare Saint-Laud. I'll be in touch with you when things are fixed."

"Will that be long?" She liked the boy, he knew. But she did not have—nor did he wish her to have—any sympathy for him. He had the feeling that were she in his place she would have told Rundell to go to hell. Somewhere in the distant past he felt it was possible that she, too, had found herself manoeuvred into the wrong line of country.

"A few days at the most." She reached for her handbag and took from it a longish, fat envelope and handed it to him. "That's for expenses."

"Thank you." He slipped the envelope into his breast pocket, and then with a wry grin, asked, "What would you have done in my place?"

Tight-lipped for a moment, she said, "You know the answer to that. And it would be better if from now on you don't open up that kind of subject again."

"O.K. Sorry."

At this moment Peter came back and said, laughing, "Eh, what do you think? I met a man fishing up there. He was English—all the way from Belsize Park!"

Miss Lloyd laughed and then said, "Did you have a chat with him?"

"No, not really. I just said I was from London."

"Did you say where in London or tell him your name?"

"No, I didn't. He was too busy grumbling about his wife and there being no fish."

*   *   *   *

They spent two days in Angers and, since the hotel had no restaurant, they ate out, except for breakfast which they had in the room they shared. Those two days Peter often found boring although his father did his best to keep him amused. He took him to some of the show places of the city—the Grand

39

Château de la Loire which was not far from their hotel, and to the Roman Arcades and the Cathedral. But his enthusiasm for such places was very modified. Two things, however, he did like. One was to walk to the river which was not far from the hotel and watch the rows of men and boys fishing. The only fishing he had ever done was in Ireland, and he thought it was something he could get to like given a proper chance. He was amused, though, to see that no one ever threw back a fish, no matter how small it was. His father told him that the French wasted nothing. Everything went into the pot.

The other thing—and this he liked more—was only a stone's throw from their hotel. This was the Gare Saint-Laud. As a station it wasn't a patch on Paddington, of course. But it was a station and there was a recognizable atmosphere about it. He made brief friends with the lady who looked after the newspaper kiosk and an old man who was repainting some of the woodwork in the main hall. Both had some English and they reminded him vaguely of May and Blackie Timms. The trains were a bit different, but there was the same feeling about them and in him as they came and went. The old man told him that he had been to London once—to Twickenham to watch a rugby international between England and France and had had his wallet stolen. He had done a lot of miming before Peter had understood the words *mon portefeuille*, and grinning had said, 'Aaaah . . . *sacrés Anglais*.' The kiosk lady spoke better English and told him how she had fallen in love with an English fighter pilot who during the War had crash-landed on her father's farm, saying, 'Only for two weeks he is with us but he goes and takes my heart with him. Since then I marry twice. But—' she grinned '—no good. You see I have no more no heart to give. When you grow up, you be good garçon and don't take somebody's heart and walk away with it.' Then giving him a big wink, she handed him a free funny paper.

It was on the evening of the day she said this that, over their evening meal in a small restaurant, his father said, "Miss Lloyd's coming for us tomorrow. You'd better put on your best suit in the morning. Also, there's something else—this gentleman whose books I'm going to look at has told Miss Lloyd that

40

he would very much like you to do your memory thing for him."

"Oh, dad—do I have to?"

"Well, it'll please him and he could be a good customer."

"You mean, if I did, you might make more money?"

"Well . . . it could tell a little." His father smiled. "In business it never is wrong to please the customer, is it?"

"No, I suppose not. Is Miss Lloyd coming?"

"Yes, she's arranged it all. She wants you to do it, too."

"Oh, well, if she wants it, too, I don't mind."

Seeing his son's face, there was for a brief moment or two a strong desire in him to pack up their things, give Miss Lloyd the slip and make their own way back to England. But the impulse died almost before he could give it any serious encouragement. He was in and there was no way of getting out now without inviting his own destruction. They would have the shop closed up within weeks and himself facing God-knew-what charges, real and false.

Maybe something of what he was feeling passed to the boy for Peter said, "Are you feeling all right, dad?"

He laughed. "Yes, of course. Well—" he patted his stomach, "—perhaps a touch of the tums. I think I tucked into those savoury pancakes a bit too freely at lunch."

"They *were* pretty super, weren't they?"

Later that evening Miss Lloyd telephoned Courtney at his hotel. She said, "I told you that we were going down to see the Comte de Servais tomorrow afternoon. But I've just had a call from him inviting us to lunch tomorrow. I'll pick you up at half-past ten. All right?"

"Why not. The sooner it's over the better."

After the call, he went slowly up to their room, wondering why he had got the impression that she was either annoyed or upset by this change in their plans.

*　　　*　　　*　　　*

The next morning Miss Lloyd called for them with her car and they drove down the valley of the Loire in the freshness of a sparkling spring morning. The poplars were in young leaf, the first rosy flush of blossom hazed the fruit trees, and on the gentle slopes men and women were working along the rows of vines.

After about thirty miles Miss Lloyd turned the car into a side road away from the river and they began to climb, twisting and turning up a gentle valley. Sitting beside her Peter wondered if, like his father, she'd eaten something which had upset her because she had little to say, and never even once made one of her jokes.

Ten minutes later they came to the gates of a château. The stone pillars each side of the gates were crowned with an eagle-kind of bird, both of them with wings half-furled. On one of the pillars was a large board with the name—Château de Servais. The driveway curled around a wooded bluff and there in front of them was the château like something out of one of the illustrations in the fairytale books from which his mother used to read to him and which now rested, well-thumbed and worn, on the bookshelf under his bedroom window at home, next to his collection of train books. It was all slated towers and turrets with narrow, pointed windows. From it a great lawn ran down to a reed-fringed lake where duck and other wildfowl moved on the waters ... and quite a few of them were fighting and chasing one another. Just like they would be doing now, he knew, on the Serpentine because the mating season was well under way.

When they stopped at the steps which ran up to a small terrace and the main door of the château, his father said, "You stay here for a while, son. Miss Lloyd and I will go and have a word with our French friend first. O.K.?"

"Yes, dad. Is it all right though if I go and have a look at the lake?"

Miss Lloyd laughed. "Absolutely, but don't fall in."

"As though I should."

When they had gone he walked down to the lake and sat on the steps of a stone temple affair with its front open pillared. Inside, above the curving run of stone bench, was a great niche holding a statue of a woman, thinly draped, who was leaning her head on one hand and looking pretty sad about something. He sat there watching the wildfowl on the lake and also the flight of swallows, dipping now and then to its surface and making rings as though fish were rising. Miss Lloyd, he thought, had been more herself this morning. But there was something about her which was different. But women, he knew, were a bit like that. Moody sometimes and you'd never know for what. His real Mum had been like that at times. And his stepmother. And May at Paddington. Now and again she would just look at him and say, 'Buzz off, Peter.' Not old Blackie, though, because he was almost always like it. He'd said once, 'Man, I got the weight of the world on mah shoulders. And what a world, full of feet and other people's trash.'

He sat there in the sun, content to watch the lake, and to pass into a day dream of his own . . . going aboard the Cornish Riviera Express. Gosh what a flyer. Sitting in the first-class. Why not? You didn't have to pay for your seat when it was all in your mind. Whumph! Whumph! That was the air suction as the express passed another flyer coming the other way. Some of the other boys at the station—though he didn't mix much with them—were funny. They just collected train numbers and knew all about bogey and driving wheels and all that. Not for him. He just liked to look at them—as he looked at people—and to dream about riding on them.

He came out of his reverie at the sound of a man's voice saying, "You must be Peter Courtney. Am I right?"

Peter stood up. "Yes, sir. I am."

The man held out a hand to him and he shook it as the other said, "And I am Alphonse Grubais. When I went to school in England the other boys called me All Grubby—which was a little bit true. I never cared much for washing in those days."

Peter laughed, and said, "My friends at school call me Bobby."

"Why?" The other looked puzzled.

"Well, you see, sir—my initials are P.C. Which stands for Police Constable and—"

"Say no more. I am with you, Bobby."

43

Monsieur Grubais laughed and Peter joined in as the man sat down by him. He liked him. He was small and neat and sort of jockey-sized. His hair which was thin, dark and flecked with grey-and-white streaks was brushed straight back, and he had a little twitch of a moustache like Charlie Chaplin. He was wearing blue trousers, a blue silk shirt with a white scarf at his throat and open-work sandals. He was pretty old, Peter guessed, for he had a worn and deeply lined face and when he wasn't smiling his expression was sad, almost miserable.

Peter said, "Is the château yours, sir?"

"Yes, it is. You see, apart from being All Grubby, I'm the Comte de Servais. My family have lived here for generations."

"Oh, you're the one my father's come to see about some books then?"

"That's right. I've left your father inside with Miss Lloyd to look over the books so that I could come and have a talk with you."

Peter said, "You want me to do my memory thing, don't you, sir?"

The Comte de Servais nodded and smiled. "Well, I wasn't intending to come to that point so fast. But yes, I would consider it a great favour. My friend Mr Rundell, whom you've met, has told me all about you. I wondered if I recited something partly in French and partly in English to you—and sent him the first lines—whether you would go with your father and see him and then ... well, you know—do the thing you do? You can do it if someone else gives you the first lines, can't you?"

"Yes, sir."

"Well, why don't we do it now? Then afterwards we'll go and have some lunch?"

"If that's what you'd like, sir. Could I just be very still and sit for a moment?"

"Make yourself comfortable."

Peter sat down on the temple step and cradled his head in his hands. It was all showmanship but he did it automatically now even though it didn't mean anything or help him at all. But it looked good and that was what his father liked. Between

44

his fingers he watched a moorhen foraging about in a patch of water lily pads. He liked the way its tail flicked now and again giving a white signal. Fussy things. Always busy about something...

He looked up after a few moments and said, "I'm ready, monsieur."

"Good. Here we go."

Slowly and deliberately the Comte de Servais began to speak in a clear, deep voice and as he spoke he raised his right hand and just gently scratched the tip of his nose.

"Il était une fois un Grand Ours qui vivait en Orient et qui avait un tas d'enfants. Quand ceux-ci grandirent ils s'en allèrent gagner leur vie dans différents pays. De temps en temps ils envoyaient à leur père des nouvelles sur les choses intéressantes qu'ils avaient vues et entendues." At this point he changed from French to English and went on, "These are their names and the addresses where they are still to be found. In France there is Monsieur Louis Turbeau of 13 Rue des Poissons, Paris. In Rome there is Signor Caspi of Flat Two, 10 Via dei Capuccini. In Germany there is...."

He went on speaking slowly and clearly while the swallows and swifts hawked over the lake, and in all listed six names before he finished. After some silence Peter took his hands from his face and, looking up, said, "Is that all, sir?"

"Yes, Peter, my friend. All and enough." The man's voice had a freshness and lightness in it which it had not had before as though, Peter thought, he had got something off his chest which had been worrying him. Grown-ups, he thought, were very funny at times. After all it was only a kind of game, a silly thing that he could do—and often wished he couldn't.

They went into the château together and from then on it was all very pleasant and interesting. They had lunch in a big conservatory where plants grew right to the roof and small tropical birds flew free ... so free that they sometimes made droppings on the table which the Comte de Servais treated as a joke, but he could see that his father and Miss Lloyd didn't think much of it. Miss Lloyd, he thought, was fidgety and clearly anxious to be away because she kept looking at her

45

watch and not eating much. For himself, he tucked in, and had two glasses of a nice white wine, while his father talked books with Monsieur le Comte. When they left he settled down in the car—on the back seat now—and soon found himself getting drowsy and finally dropped off to sleep as the wine worked in him.

He didn't wake until the car stopped outside their hotel and he heard Miss Lloyd say to his father, "I'll pick you up tomorrow morning. With luck you'll be able to get one of the afternoon boats." Then she turned to him and with one of her nice smiles said in her old teasing, pleasant tone, "You've been a super chap, Peter. But if I were you I'd lay off the wine until you're a little older. Did you know you snored in your sleep?"

He laughed. "Yes, Miss Lloyd. My father bangs the wall when I do, and then I stop—so he says."

Miss Lloyd drove off, and they went up to their room to have a wash and tidy up, and Peter said, "Can I pop over to the station to say goodbye to my friends since we're going tomorrow?"

"You want to?"

"Yes, please."

"O.K. And Peter—"

"Yes?"

"You behaved jolly well. I was proud of you."

"Oh ... well. He was a nice man. Are you going to buy some of his books?"

"I think I may."

When the boy was gone he sat in the window and looked down at the traffic moving along the Rue Denis Papin, feeling drained and too tired to do more than acknowledge the growing disgust he felt for himself. Everything had gone all right, but there was no escaping the fact that today he had moved, taking his son with him, into a new world. Well, one thing for sure was that it would never happen again. Once he had his money that would be an end of it. He would wipe Mr Rundell and his world from his mind, and there would be no more dragging Peter around to do his parlour game. Absolutely not. Finish. Finish. Finish.

46

Some little time after his guests had gone the Comte de Servais walked down to the lake temple. The early afternoon sun was casting fast-moving cloud shadows across its waters. He felt drained but at ease. He had done now what he had long contemplated. He had some days before telephoned to his friend Rundell the opening French lines of his speech to the memory boy—as he already had named him to himself. Rundell now had a key with which to open up the list of names of those who had and were still betraying their countries— some from secret political convictions and some for gold.

He thought of the boy who had recently been here in the temple talking to him and the memory was overlaid by another and much older one . . . of another boy, his own, who had often sat here with him, swum in the lake and eaten in the big conservatory and had not minded the birds any more than the other had. A son who had grown to a young man, become an agent in the French intelligence service and had been tortured and then murdered by the Russians in East Berlin. Since then he had worked and waited long to take revenge on the Russian Bear. Now he had done so, and knew without fear that some day, unless he were very lucky, the bear would come lumbering after him to maul him to death. Wearing nothing over his blue silk shirt he shivered a little in the chill wind that had risen over the lake waters.

Then, as though both he and the other were merely actors playing a part, the dramatic surprise precisely timed, a man came quietly around the side of the temple and stood at the bottom of the steps looking up at him. He had never seen the man before but he knew the reason of his coming because it rested unwaveringly in his right hand—a hand which, he recognized in a moment of intense clarity and also because he had loved all firearms since a youth, held a Walther P.P.K. automatic pistol.

The man said politely, "Good day, monsieur. I am sorry to tell you that you will be unable to greet the visitors you expect this afternoon."

The Comte de Servais shrugged his shoulders and said, "That is a pity then. But there is no questioning the will of God." He raised his hand and crossed himself.

The man fired twice, the sound of the shots sending the water fowl rising from the lake. Then he turned and ran for the cover of the nearby shrubberies. The Comte de Servais lay crumpled awkwardly on the top step of the temple, its white marble reddening with blood, as the echoes of the shots died away in the far woods and set the water fowl into panic flight.

*　　*　　*　　*

Christopher Lang sat at the kitchen table, the suitcase he had just carried in from the taxi on the floor at his side, and watched Joan making coffee for him.

He said cheerfully, "In France, eh? What's he doing over there—and with the boy?"

"I dunno. Gone to look at some books he might handle for sale, I think. You know Frank—he never says much about his business."

Chris laughed. "Just as well, perhaps. He's no porno chap, I know—and I guess you do—but I always get the feeling he's . . . well, a tiny bit on the shady side. No?"

"He's as straight as a die."

He laughed. "Then he's dead." As she brought him his coffee and set it down, he patted and fondled her bottom, and asked, "When are they coming back?"

"I don't know that either. Two, three days, maybe. He said he'd ring from Southampton."

"Well, that's nice, isn't it? We can settle down for a while like we used to be—still are, in fact—a cosy married couple. No hole and corner stuff in the afternoon while he's at work and the boy's at school."

"I don't know about that."

"Oh, yes you do. And when they're back we'll still manage."

"I don't know about that, either . . ."

"Oh, yes you do. I'll be here for at least a month."

"A month!"

He laughed. "You should see your face! Yes, a month. They've got some old tub up at Gourock having a refit and when she's ready they're giving me first engineer. But until then I'm on paid leave. And after the Red Sea and the bloody Gulf, and stinking scum yelling away for backsheesh every step, I'm ready for some fun." His voice was suddenly serious. "But don't fret. I'm not going to step out of line when he or the boy is around, as you know. No need to spoil things, is there? So, put a big smile on your face and think of happy times ahead."

"It's not right. I've never liked it."

"Don't give me that. He's no good to you the way I am, and you know it and like me to do something about it. Now then—" he reached for his case, put it on the table and began to open it, "—let's see what nice present a good boy has brought for a good girl."

CHAPTER FOUR

RUNDELL SAT IN the window seat of his office, looking out
across the Thames and listening to the notes of Big Ben striking the hour as the early evening traffic streamed along the far
Embankment. There was a knock on his door and in answer to
his call Edward Tampion came in.

Rundell gave him a friendly smile. He liked Teddy
Tampion. Underneath his rather modish, silly-ass manner
there lay disguised another Tampion, a man with a first-class
brain, iron nerves, and the itch of ambition.

"Evening, Teddy. I was just thinking of moving off."

"I bring news, sir—sweet and sour, I'm afraid. Miss Lloyd
has just come through. She did the Comte de Servais thing this
morning instead of this afternoon."

"Why?"

Tampion said, "At his request. And it was as well, too. A
little while ago she says that the French radio broke the news
that he was assassinated this afternoon."

"Good God ... poor old chap."

"It was always on the cards with his background ...
Anyway, the boy and his father will be here tomorrow. They
know nothing about it. There's no line that can lead to them—
thank the Lord. Queer little sprout, the boy. I really quite took
to him. Pappa? Ah, well—he could jolly well be a horse of a different colour. Somewhere along the line there the wires got
tangled up."

"That could be said of a lot of people."

"True, sir. Sad about de Servais. How the devil did they get
on to him, I wonder?"

Rundell shrugged his shoulders. "The world is over-littered

with unanswerable questions..."

Tampion, fingering the signet ring he wore on his right hand, laughed briefly. "Which came first the chicken or the jolly old egg, what?"

With a sudden asperity, roused a little by Tampion's manner, he said, "If anything had happened to that boy, I know that I could never forgive myself. People like us know the risks we take. And the boy's father ... well, he's got enough sense to know when the shades of grey begin to turn black." He laughed, suddenly and harshly. "Perhaps my father was right. He wanted me to go into the Church."

Tampion laughed with him and said, "Ditto my pater, too. Only he was for the Guards. But how can you when you not only hate horses but they give you jolly old asthma as well?"

Rundell stood up. "I'm going to my club."

"A calm backwater in a stormy world."

Fifteen minutes after Rundell had left the office Tampion followed. He walked across Vauxhall Bridge and then took a taxi to Knightsbridge. The evening was calm and balmy. Bowler-hatted and swinging his impeccably furled umbrella, dark-suited and hissing a gentle tune through his teeth, he walked into Hyde Park. He found a seat near the Serpentine, parked his umbrella between his knees, and shook out his evening paper.

After a while a man came along the gravelly path and sat down a few feet from him. He wore a green-and-brown Army camouflaged windbreaker, brown canvas trousers and open-work sandals over his bare feet. He pulled a tobacco tin from his pocket and rolled himself a cigarette with heavily nicotined fingers. Leaning back he began to smoke and stared skyward to watch the slow drift of the light evening clouds across the sunset-reddened sky. After a while he said, "I'm in. Three days ago. First-floor flat—not much of a place. Self-contained. Good angles. I'm almost dead opposite the boy's house. Shouldn't be any problem. Do I take them both?"

Tampion shook out his paper and turned a page. Looking straight ahead he said, "You take the boy first, and then the father. It's the boy we want. The father's nothing. *The boy first.*" The last three words were harsh with near anger.

"Whatever?"

"Yes. The boy first."

"When?"

"Tomorrow. Any time from midday on."

"O.K."

"When I get up you'll see I've left something for you."

Tampion gave his paper a shake and folded it. Putting it under his arm he stood up and began to walk away, swinging his umbrella. The man reached over and picked up an envelope on which Tampion had been sitting. It was warm to his touch. He opened it. Inside were two photographs—one of the boy and one of the father, both head and shoulders. The boy looked a nice sort of kid ... windbreaker, hair a little ruffled, big smile. Without any sentiment he thought ... *bit like sister Alice's kid.* Christ—what would she have thought about all this? The man ... well, he looked fairly ordinary. Bit of seediness about him, though. Lost a pound and found a penny. Wonder what the hell it was all about? Who cared, anyway? The money was good. He stood up, put the photographs in his pocket, and began to walk away towards the tennis courts and the bridge over the Serpentine.

*   *   *   *

Since there was no restaurant in their hotel, they had gone out to dinner. When they got back late the receptionist at the desk handed Courtney a message which read—*Important. Ring Miss Lloyd immediately. Hotel Concorde. Tel: 88.63.19. Urgent.*

While his father telephoned, Peter went up to their room and got into bed. When his father came up, he asked, "What was it, Dad?" He could see that his father looked a bit upset and almost angry.

"It was our bossy Miss Lloyd."

Peter laughed. "She is a bit, isn't she? Just now and then. But underneath she's very nice, I think."

Courtney forced himself to laugh. "Well, you won't think so when I tell you that she wants us to get an early boat from

Cherbourg. She's calling for us at five o'clock tomorrow morning to drive us up there. And there'll be a car waiting for us in Southampton to take us to London."

"Well, that's all right, isn't it? I quite like getting up early. That's what Mum used to say, wasn't it? If you want the best of the day then be up at . . ."

Despite his own mood Courtney laughed. "Go on, I know what she used to say."

"Be up at sparrow-fart before the world gets clogged with people."

Courtney laughed, feeling the irritation in him fading. It was not all she used to say. *Each morning is a fresh beginning and God watches, full of His everlasting hope that we'll take Christian advantage of it*. Anyway, he would be glad to get out of this country. Wished now, in fact, that he had never come. Well, this was the end. There had been nothing about this business that he had liked and when they got back there was going to be an end to it all. No more demonstrations, no more dragging Peter around as though he were some freak at a fair. And now—to have to be off at five o'clock! And her excuse—that after she had dropped them—she had to drive on to Paris to attend to some other urgent business.

Suddenly from the darkness Peter chuckled and said, "What do you think Joannie would say if we had budgerigars and African finches flying round the dining room?"

"She'd pack her bags and go." He laughed, but there was no true humour in him. Just at this moment he would like to pack his and the boy's bags and go . . . away, anywhere. Aye, back into the past if he could . . . begin again from some point where there had been no Mr Rundell or Miss Lloyd, and no memory exhibitions. Christ, something had happened to him after Sarah went. And Miss Lloyd . . . he couldn't swear to it, but for a while there had been something in her voice which had unsettled him. She had been cool and calm enough, but in every word there had been an edge and she had given her instructions as though she had only to crack the whip and he and Peter would dance for her. It was a long time before he fell asleep.

53

Miss Lloyd drove like the wind, a hard, concentrated professional exhibition, yet taking few risks, and obviously not in the mood for conversation. She had brought a large thermos of coffee and some croissants for them. For herself, she ate nothing. After eating, Peter curled up in the back seat and went to sleep for an hour.

They arrived in Cherbourg just after nine o'clock. Before they went aboard the ferry his father left them to buy a paper. Miss Lloyd turned to Peter and said, "Well, I hope you have a good crossing, Peter. Have you enjoyed yourself?"

"Oh, yes, Miss Lloyd. Well, all except getting up so early."

"I'm sorry about that. But I have to get on to Paris for an important meeting."

"I didn't mind really." Then after a pause he went on, "What do you do for a living, Miss Lloyd?"

She laughed and said, "I'm a dog's-body for a very big company. What do you want to do when you grow up?"

"I dunno."

"Engine driver?"

"Oh, no. I like trains and stations—but I wouldn't want it for work. It's better to have that on the side . . . to go to to forget other things. Something will turn up, I suppose."

"I'm sure it will. Probably something you never even thought of."

"Did that happen to you?"

She was silent for a moment, and then she put out a hand and rubbed his nose gently. "Yes, something like that, I suppose you could say."

Sometime later, as she watched the ferry pull away from its berth and make for the open sea and before she turned to go to her car, she thought—How did it happen to you? It was hard to remember exactly. Little by little, step by step, the whole thing had just wrapped itself around her.

There was a stiff breeze blowing when they found themselves outside the harbour. Courtney went into the lounge to read the paper he had bought. He had only been able to buy a French one and with his poor French he knew he was going to get little joy from it. Peter had stayed on deck to wander

54

around. Courtney lit himself a cigarette and unfolded the paper. As he looked at the front page the shock he got made him say aloud—"Christ Almighty!"

A big headline announced—*Le Comte de Servais brutalement assassiné.* Following that was a very brief news paragraph, giving few details of the murder, but he made out enough of the sense to gather what had happened. He got up, shaking with shock and anger, and went to one of the litter bins. He screwed up the paper and dropped it in. He went back and sat down and slowly pulled himself together. For the moment he could not think rationally. The only thing he could see clearly was that Miss Lloyd must have long had the news—perhaps over the radio last night at her hotel—and then her one thought would have been to get himself and Peter out of the country as quickly as possible.

He sat there, fighting down his emotions and angry thoughts—and there was a hard core of self-disgust in him because he had let himself become involved in all this for money. Rundell had talked him into it—and talked him in easily because, he had to admit, there had been less in the polite hints of trouble to be made for him at the book shop than the appeal of easy money. And he had dragged Peter with him. Now what did he do? The answer to that came quickly and inescapably. There was nothing he could damn well do. They had him and he had to go along with them. Had to. There was just one hope—that once Peter had passed on whatever the Comte had said to him—they would honour their side of the bargain. Pay up and let them go back to the obscurity from which they had come. Dear God ... that *had* to happen. Had to happen.

He got up and went to the bar and ordered a large brandy. As he stood there, his drink half-finished, Peter came up to him, hair tousled by the wind, his cheeks damp with blown spray.

Peter smiled at him. "I know what's in that glass. I can always tell the smell. Brandy, isn't it?"

"Yes, it is. I began to feel a little queasy."

"Well, it's good stuff to take for sea-sickness. I know that

55

from Grandfather Patrick."

"How?" Somehow with the boy at his side now, the loneliness of spirit and self-disgust eased.

"Well, when he took me fishing on the lough he was always taking a swallow from his bottle so I asked him why he did it. And he said, 'Water upsets me belly, boy—particularly when it moves about so much. Tis no sea-sickness, mind you—just the damned persistence of the elements upsetting a man until he needs a little comfort.' He gave me a sip, you know. It was awful."

Courtney laughed and the sound was strange in his own ears. The boy's face was all innocence and—God help him—full of Sarah. He said, "Your grandpa's a great leg-puller." And more than that—as straight as a die. Were he here now he would have murdered him for dragging the boy into God knew what trouble to come if things went wrong.

They were met at Southampton as they came out of Customs by a uniformed chauffeur holding a board with the name *Mr Frank Courtney* on it.

As they drove off Peter said, "Gosh, this is real posh treatment, isn't it?"

The driver half turned his head, grinned, and said, "That's our motto—do things in style for them as deserves it. And I can tell you there aren't all that many of 'em about. The world is going to the dogs and I wouldn't be surprised if in the end we all found ourselves living in kennels—which in its way, of course, would be bad luck on the real dogs for decenter and more lovin' creatures there's none to be found."

Peter laughed and said, "You sound like my grandfather."

The man chuckled. "Then he can only be one thing—a Paddy like myself. And I'll be guessin' too that it's a half Paddy you must be yourself for your father's clearly set in the mould of an honest English gentleman."

And so the talk went, on and off, all the way to London and it was some time before Courtney came to the conclusion that the choice of driver must have been Mr Rundell's so that the boy could be kept amused. Which was a point in his favour—and he hoped that there would be other points too so that he would let Peter speak his memory lines and then leave them both alone in peace. Never again should the boy ever perform. This was the end. By all the saints he swore it.

*   *   *   *

A little before half-past five he settled himself by the run of lace-curtained windows. One of the lattice windows was six inches open on the catch, the curtain stirring slightly in the light breeze. Across the road from him was the Courtney house and from the height of his room he had a clear view of the tiled run up to the front door above which hung a moss-lined hanging basket with plants in it. Nice house, neat, respectable. Like all the others. And all keeping to themselves. Not wanting to know about anyone else. The boy first—the father next if he still was fool enough to stand and be an easy target. *But the boy first*. That was the order. One shot. Maybe two at the most and then he would be away. Fifty yards to go through all the fuss and bother and confusion. Thank the Lord for confusion. It fuddled people's brains and eyes. And then the car for Heathrow and sunny Spain waiting round the corner. The old woman downstairs in her kitchen probably wouldn't hear a thing. Radio going full tilt all day and nearly half the night. He gave the tight surgical gloves on his hands an easing stretch. No finger prints anywhere in the flat—that had been a bore. But there—the price was good and took care of that little inconvenience.

He squatted down on the stool below the window and picked up the rifle they had supplied him with. It was a rebuilt S.M.L.E. from the old No. 4 World War Two rifle. Sporting caterpillar foresight. Standard and two-leafed rear-sight. Cheapish compared to some. But good enough for this job. They watched the money and knew that he would have to leave it. But it would do the job ... Oh, yes, in his hands it would do the job. Spain and the dolly-birds waiting. Nothing to do but enjoy himself until the money ran out—and there was always more where that came from.

He watched a mongrel dog come down the road, cocking its

57

leg now and then against a hub cap. Go on for hours they could—where did it all come from? There was a car parked outside the house. Cars parked everywhere along the road. But no matter, he had a clear view of the front path, two steps and the door.... Anything goes wrong—like they don't turn up—just sit tight till the phone goes down in the hall and the old girl shouts up—"Someone for you." Bugger about these gloves. Stopped a man smoking. But there it was. Some sacrifices had to be made for the sake of the good times ahead.

He looked at his wristwatch. Half-past four. They had said most likely some time between four and six. But he was conscientious, if only on account of the money involved, and he had been sitting here since three o'clock. They hadn't been able to give him a car number, only that it would be an official car, chauffeur driven. That chap in the Park—bowler hat and umbrella—you wouldn't think to look at him that he could be mixed up in anything like this. You wouldn't think it—but it didn't really surprise you. Not these days. Saints and sinners ... you couldn't tell them by their dress. He grinned at the thought, and then the grin went quickly from his face.

Some way up the street he had seen the car. Daimler. Chauffeur driven. Had to be. Instinct was as good as truth in him. He settled easily into a firing position and waited as the car came slowly down the street and then pulled up in the road abreast of the car which was already parked outside the house. The chauffeur got out and was quickly around to open the rear door on the house side. He reached in and took out a large suitcase. He put it on the ground and then fumbled in his pocket and pulled out a big white envelope which he handed to a man who had got out of the car. The chauffeur made a gesture to carry the case to the house but the man shook his head and picked up the case himself. As the chauffeur got back into the Daimler the man went round the back of the parked car and up the tiled paving to the door. He put the case down for a moment, took a key from his pocket, unlocked the door and went in with his case. As the door closed behind him the Daimler pulled away and went down the street.

He stayed kneeling at the window, his rifle still lined up

Then with a sudden spurt of irritation, near anger, he said, "What the bloody hell? Where's the boy?" Then, slowly, his frustration ebbed. There was nothing he could do. His instructions had been clear. If he did the job he was to go—fast. If anything went wrong he was to sit tight unless his own safety was involved. They would ring eventually, and if he wasn't there to answer they would know the job had been done. Well ... the job hadn't been done. Not yet. But where was the bloody boy? He put the rifle on the floor carefully and then slipped off his gloves. Whether they liked it or not he was going to have a smoke. Flick the ash out of the window and the stub after it.

*   *   *   *

Frank Courtney put his case at the foot of the stairs and then slipped into his jacket pocket the fat envelope which the chauffeur had given him. The house was quiet. He went through to the kitchen. It was neat and tidy. Joan must be out. In a way he was glad. Give him time to settle down, to let the last few days ease from him. He was glad to be back but there was tiredness in him like a slow ache. He was tempted to get himself a drink but resisted the desire. In his pocket—no need to count them—were two thousand pounds. By the feel of it they had to be fifty pound notes. Forty of them ... and the Comte de Servais was dead... What he needed now was a bath and a change. But it wouldn't make any difference. Fresh clothes and a well-bathed body would still leave him Frank Courtney. Later, perhaps, a few whiskies would bring the illusion of peace of mind. Well, if you couldn't have real peace you had to take what substitute you could find.

He turned back into the carpeted hall, picked up his suitcase, and slowly climbed the stairs. He put the case down outside the bedroom door and went in.

The fast-lowering western sun struck a long parallelogram of bright light down the middle of the room and fell boldly across the bottom of the far single bed. For a moment or two he stood there, and oddly enough—although he felt anger rising in him—there was no surprise. Suddenly dozens of small incidents, past ambiguous scraps of talk, and perhaps some kind of animal instinct combined to make the reality which faced him almost acceptable. Acceptable as fact, as though he had long known it. But nevertheless something which struck at his tattered self-pride and the miserable disarray of his manhood.

They were together in the far single bed, the covers partly off them. Chris lay on his back, his naked sun-browned chest matted with dark hairs against which the fair hair of Joan made sharp, golden contrast as she lay partly drawn to him in the crook of his bent left arm. In the moments of the startling clarity of his growing understanding ... memories of odd moments of doubt littering his mind from the past ... he found the flattened mis-shaping of the fall of her left breast against Chris's arm grotesque and sordid. Whorish ... the word swam gently into his mind. Whore, too, she was. But some things, he knew, were even beyond her. She would never have gone to bed with her brother. It was no brother that lay in the bed with her. This was the end. He could never stay here, never bring Peter back to this house, and for himself never find need to wake them and get entangled in explanations or promises for the future. At this moment Joan stirred in her sleep and half-giggled in the pleasure of some dream. The sound was obscene and he turned quietly away and went out of the room, knowing that this was not the end for him. Now he was an animal, turning away, to seek any shelter to lick the wounds suffered by his spirit and self-pride.

He went downstairs, suffering, but not caring a damn. Neither he nor Peter would ever enter the house again. No matter what. No matter how it had to be arranged. Time would come for thinking. The time now was for flight ... from them, and from his past, and from himself ...

Downstairs he was tempted to pause and write some kind of note and leave it on the kitchen table. But anger suddenly made him reject the idea. He owed them nothing. The house was hers and she could whore in it to her heart's content.

He went out of the house and shut the door quietly. Carrying his suitcase he turned right-handed up the road towards

Praed Street. On their way back as they had come along the Bayswater Road Peter had asked if he could be dropped off at Paddington Station. He remembered the Daimler driver turning to him as they drove off after leaving the boy, and saying, "Mad about trains, is he?"

He had smiled. "Dotty..."

"Oh, I don't know, sir. Better than pinching old ladies' handbags or larkin' about with girls because they think they're old enough to know what they've got it for. Kids ... these days!"

He turned into Praed Street, keeping his eyes open for his son. Thank God he knew his route and all his calling points. Peter had told him all about them. And anyway, if he missed him, he'd park his case at the station and go back and fetch him. Face them, but no being put off. At the station he went in through the hotel entrance. Peter had friends on the desk. He'd make a call here. But there was no Peter.

He went through to the station concourse and then—remembering May he went on to her kiosk. He waited until the customers cleared and then said, "I'm Peter Courtney's father. I left him here and said I'd pick him up. Have you seen him?"

May gave him a smile. "One look at you and I can tell you're his father. Yes, he's been here. Full of inky-pinky parly-voo and how they run things on French stations. He just went up the platform to look for Blackie Timms, he's the—"

"Thank you. Yes, I know who Blackie is. Thanks very much."

"Be my guest."

He found him almost at the far end of the platform talking to one of the station cleaners—Blackie Timms.

Peter, surprised to see him, said, "What are you doing here, Dad?"

"I've come for you. I want to talk to you."

"You look ... well, is something wrong?"

Blackie Timms, scarcely looking up, said, "Man—something's nearly always wrong. And if it don't look that kinda way—Man, it soon turns out to be. I knows that. I married one I marked for da sweetest angel in the whole cosmonaut. But it none o' my business to load you wi' the way she turned out to be wasn't. You go off wid yuh pappy. He looks kind o' worried.''

As Courtney took Peter by the arm and led him away, the boy said, "Are you worried? Is something wrong?"

He smiled. "Not really. Just something's happened. I'll tell you about it later. But for the moment, I want you to do something for me."

"What?"

"Well, you know all the trains that go from here—so, I want you to choose one that's going fairly soon and we'll get on it."

"Just like that?"

"Well, why not? I feel like it. And you'd like it, wouldn't you?"

"Well, yes. But what about Joan and all the rest?"

"That's all fixed. We can just go off, anywhere you pick. For as long as we like. No bother with school or anything like that. Come on now!" He felt the swift rise of irritation and frustration touch him. "Just pick a damned train and we'll go!"

"You mean I can pick *any* train I like?"

"Any—and as a treat we'll go first class."

"First class? Did you win the pools or something?"

"Yes ... something."

Peter suddenly grinned. "Well—that's easy. I'd like to go on one of the high-speed trains ... say, to Bristol or Exeter or even further on than that." He paused and then said slowly, "First class—I say, that's really something, isn't it?"

"And so it should be. We're going to have a super time."

*   *   *   *

He heard the telephone ringing, then the shuffle of the old girl's sloppy slippers along the hall, and finally her voice calling, "It's for you, Mister Jones."

He went down to the hall, picked up the receiver and waited until the old lady was back in her kitchen with the ever-playing radio.

He said, "Yes?"

"Why are you still there?"

"The father came back in the car. But no boy. Then after a while he came out, carrying his case and walked off ... up towards Praed Street. What do you want me to do?"

"Stay put so long as the light lasts."

"And then?"

"Stay there until I ring again "

"They might never be back."

"Don't be a damned fool. They live there."

His caller rang off.

*　　*　　*　　*

He bought two first-class single tickets for Exeter. By the time they got there it would be late and there was no point in tiring the boy with a longer journey. Christ, the day had been long enough already, getting up at five. Then they went into the hotel and had coffee and biscuits. From the desk he got paper and envelopes and wrote two letters.

The first was to Jensen, who was looking after the book shop for him. He told him that he had had a call to go away on business again for some time. He hoped he wouldn't mind carrying on for a while. He could draw his wages from the takings. He would be in touch again very soon. Jensen wouldn't mind, he knew. He lived with a widowed sister in a state of frequently broken harmony. The shop was his refuge. Now he could seek it every day.

The second letter was harder to write, but little longer, and baldly put.

I came back and found you and Chris asleep in the same bed. If he is your brother, may God forgive you. But I don't think he is. I grant you that much decency. The place is yours. I shan't tell Peter about this.

He paused for a while, undecided how to go on and then he added:

63

If Chris lets you down, you can get money from Jensen at the shop until I can get things properly squared up through lawyers or whatever. I don't ever want to see you again, nor for the boy to either.

He signed it *Frank Courtney*, got stamps from the girl at the reception desk and dropped the letters into their mail box. As he did so the girl at the desk said, "You must be Mr Courtney, no?"

"Yes. How could you know?"

She smiled. "That's your boy over there. You both got the same look. We all know Peter." She nodded at the exposed parts of the two train tickets he had pushed into his breast pocket, and went on, "Going for a trip?"

"Yes, we are."

"That'll please him. Going far?"

"Well, just around. Exeter tonight and then ... well, who knows? The wide open spaces."

"Lucky you."

"I know..."

When he got back to Peter, the boy said, "She's nice, isn't she. Nicer than the others, anyway. They go for me when I take a short cut through here. But not today they can't." He slowly flexed his arms and gave a small yawn. "Gosh, it's been a day, hasn't it? All the way from France and now this."

Looking at his son he slowly smiled. This at least was his. His own flesh and blood. Trusting, loving, knowing that he would be looked after and protected. And as near as a touch he had damned nearly spoiled that for good. Begun to use him to feed his own bruised ego and for the sake of a few miserable pounds now and again. Sarah would have murdered him ... but that wouldn't have been enough. There would have had to have been slow torture first and then a long agony of dying.

*   *   *   *

Working late, Mr Rundell from his desk in the window

looked out over the river. The Embankment lights threw broken reflections on the dark river, and somewhere distantly he could hear the clanging of an ambulance's emergency bell. Some old lady, he thought, in her single room falling asleep from the fumes of an inefficient oil stove... Some girl typist homeward bound full of love's young dreams, taking a chance to cross the crowded road and death waiting for her as one of her shoe heels broke and toppled her into the path of a car with bad brakes driven by some idiot taking stupid risks to get home in time to catch the beginning of some worthless television show... In the midst of life we are in death. The Comte de Servais, with whom he had shared many a brew-up at Wellington as a boy, would have known that and been prepared, philosophical. For some men there came a time in life when they knew that deliberately designed death could come at any moment. He, himself, and many others in this building knew it.

He reached for his internal telephone and called Teddy Tampion.

"Teddy—any news?"

"No, sir. The chauffeur said the boy was dropped off at Paddington Station. That's his thing. Trains. And then he took Courtney home. Not far away, as you know. He paid him off and saw him go into the house with his suitcase. Then he drove off."

"And since then?"

"We've phoned twice to the house for him and his wife said he's not there."

"Was she worried?"

"No. She said she wasn't expecting him home yet and that he was on a trip to France. I didn't linger over it the second time because she seemed to be a bit fussed at being called again."

"Quite right. Odd, ain't it?"

Tampion laughed and drawled, "Curiouser and curiouser, as Alice said. We know he went in and we know she was there—and yet she says she hasn't seen him."

"All right. We'll leave it for a bit. I'll have to take some advice on it."

"Yes, sir."

In his room Tampion put down his receiver, leaned back in his chair, and smiled to himself, thinking, *That's right. You leave it. But not me.* An hour ago he had gone out to a telephone kiosk and put in a call to an ex-directory number and without any preamble, except the phrase—*Stormbird here*—had said, "Call that thug off from across the road, and get a man fast to Paddington. I've an idea the boy and his father may be taking a train somewhere. If he spots them tell him to follow and report. No more than that. Just report."

Putting down the receiver he had thought—'If I knew for sure that my name wasn't on the Comte's list I'd be a happy man.'

CHAPTER FIVE

HE WAS AWAKE early. Lying in bed, sunlight flooding into the room since they had drawn the curtains back before going to sleep, he could hear through the partly open window the noise of traffic outside and also, now and again, the sound of a train's siren going as it came through non-stop at the station which was just across the square from the hotel. Lovely sound, he thought. In fact everything was lovely, though a bit puzzling. Still, at the moment, there was no need to fuss over that. His father would make all that clear some time.

He lay there, thinking of the train they had come West on ... high-speed, non-stop to Taunton and then on to Exeter where they had got off, though he would have liked to stick with it all the way down to Penzance. But his father was tired and so was he so they had got off and walked across the square to this hotel. Would have been better, though, if they could have made the run in daylight, but the dusk was thickening as they had pulled out of Paddington. First class, sitting in the Smoking section of the coach, with a carton of orange for himself and whisky for his father, fetched from the buffet—and soon they were going to have dinner in the restaurant car ... He went back over it all, and the excitement and pleasure he had known then rose again in him, not so intense, but in a way that made him feel good, so good, that to ease it he stretched his legs deep into the bottom of the bed and braced his shoulders against the slow spasm of pleasure still with him. The darkness had come too soon but it had only brought with it a new dimension of delight. The lights of towns and villages and the wailing, wailing of the train's call as they sped non-stop through stations. It was a lovely sound ... lovely, lovely.

So good was everything that he could feel even now that he might be in a dream. That in a moment or two he would really wake up and find himself back in his proper bed . . . He'd had gammon and chips and a piece of apple pie—and his father the same. But none of the wine his father had ordered. Just water. And when he had asked how long they were going for his father had just grinned and said that was in the lap of the gods. The thing to do was not to look too far ahead and to just enjoy themselves . . . which was all right with him. But it still left it a bit up in the air. And something must have happened. Because things didn't just take off like this as though it was just a normal thing that happened every day to people. When he had asked his father whether Joannie knew, he had said she did and everything was all right there. Well, he hoped it was. But somehow he didn't think it was. Anyway, when his father wanted him to know he would tell him. Probably they might have had a quarrel. Not that they often did. Anyway, grownups were odd. You just had to bear with them sometimes and keep your fingers crossed that you didn't say the wrong thing. They all changed at times—*snap*, like that. All of them . . . Miss Lloyd, May and Blackie, and the masters at school. Snap—and suddenly they were quite different.

His father woke and said sleepily, "What's going on inside that head of yours?"

"Oh, nothing much. What are we going to do today?"

"What would you like to do?"

"You mean I can choose?"

"Within reason." His father laughed. "Don't ask to go to the North Pole though."

"No, I don't want to go there. But—if it's a holiday—could we get on the train again?"

"Why not?"

"Where to?"

"Well, as far as it goes if you like. Westwards, Penzance . . . and right on, but from there you'll have to walk until you fall off the tip of Land's End. Suit you?"

Peter laughed. "Yes, it does—all except the falling off."

"Well, that's what we'll do then. You're the one with the

68

timetable. You'd better look up a train—but give us time to have a decent breakfast first."

*   *   *   *

Chris had gone off early because he had an appointment at the London office of his shipping line. Joan sat at the uncleared breakfast table in the kitchen in her dressing gown and slippers, the *Daily Mail* propped against the marmalade jar and a fresh cup of coffee at her side to go with her first cigarette of the day. In a little while she would go upstairs to dress properly and do her hair and face. At the moment she felt relaxed and at peace with the world. Well, almost at peace ... every little while the thought of Chris disturbed her. He hadn't said anything, but she could sense the change in him. Now that he was going to be here for some time she knew that he was going to find Frank hard to take. Jealousy, that's what it was. And natural, too, she supposed. When he came back for a few days, a week at the most, there was no trouble. Time was too short. But a month was a bit much. Night after night sleeping in the spare room and knowing that she and Frank were together in the next room. And he wouldn't take it from her that it only happened once in a blue moon. Well, there was nothing she could do about it. If he didn't like it he would have to lump it.

At this moment she heard the letter-box flap click and the short ring on the bell which meant the postman. She went into the hall, tightening the waistcord of her dressing gown, and picked up the one letter which lay on the mat.

Back in the kitchen she sat down and opened it. She read it and then re-read it and then sat very still, staring out of the kitchen window at a patch of rain-grey sky showing over the high towers of a great block of flats. Then slowly she gave an anguished groan that sounded more animal than human. The cigarette in her still hand burnt down and seared her fingers, the pain bringing her to life. She stubbed the end out. Reality imposed itself, easing her from shock. In her heart she had known that one day it would happen. And now it was here. There was nothing she could do about it. She knew Frank too well to think that he would ever go back on his word—and why should he? She and Chris had treated him like dirt. What Chris would think or do about it meant nothing to her. One thing he would have to face was that he was her legal husband still and had knowingly let it all happen. Frank and the boy would never return to this house. That she knew.

She went up to the bedroom and dressed herself. Not thinking. Moving like an automaton. Taking the sheets off the one disturbed bed because it was laundry day. Still not thinking of the future. Just this day which would have to be lived through before there was need to consider the future . . . this day which would hold Chris's return and then he, too, would have to share the mess of her life and do something about it because without him this day would never have been running the course already set for her by it.

As she went downstairs the front door bell rang again. She opened it to find a young woman wearing a red beret over her dark hair, and a smart, belted white raincoat.

The caller said, "Mrs Courtney?"

"Yes."

"I'm Miss Lloyd. Perhaps you've heard of me?"

To her surprise Joan felt pleasure and some relief just to talk to someone, anyone, and she said, putting on a smile, "Yes, I have—through Peter. He was full of you and going to France."

"I'd like to talk to you. Could I come in?"

"Of course."

She went ahead and led Miss Lloyd into the sitting room. She was annoyed to see that Chris had left his empty whisky glass from last night perched on the arm of one of the easy chairs. She picked it up and held it to herself as she said, "Please sit down."

Miss Lloyd sat down in a chair by the fireplace and Joan said, "What can I do for you, Miss Lloyd?"

"Well, you know I took Peter and your husband to France to do some business about books for Mr Rundell, don't you?"

"Yes." She sat nursing the glass to herself.

"And that someone from our office phoned last evening wanting to speak to him and you answered it and said he

70

wasn't here?"

"Yes, I did and..." she hesitated, feeling her lips quiver uncontrollably.

"And what, Mrs Courtney?" asked Miss Lloyd softly.

Joan closed her eyes momentarily, tightening her lids to keep tears back. Then she put her hand into one of her cardigan pockets, pulled out Frank Courtney's letter and passed it to Miss Lloyd without a word.

Miss Lloyd read it, feeling immediate sympathy for the woman and knowing that she needed to be treated gently. She said sympathetically, "Would you like to tell me about it?"

"Oh, I would!" Her words were almost vehement. "I feel if I don't tell someone about it I'll collapse in a heap and never pull myself together again."

Miss Lloyd went to her and took the glass she was holding and then walked to the window and with her back to the woman said, "I think it would be a good and helpful thing if you told me all about it. You can rely on my confidence."

It all came out then. At first she spoke hurriedly and a little incoherently and then, calming down, her voice steadied.

"... you can see from the letter. He came here and found Chris and me in bed asleep. He's not my brother, Miss Lloyd. He was ... well, still is legally my husband. But when I married Frank I didn't know he wasn't dead ..."

Miss Lloyd put the glass down on the window table and went to her and put a hand comfortingly on her shoulder. She said, "I'm beginning to see. I'm so sorry for you, Mrs Courtney. What will happen when ... well, your real husband comes back?"

With a quick flash of spirit, Mrs Courtney said, "Well, he'll just have to measure up to it, won't he? We're man and wife, whether he likes it or not. He's had the best of things so far ... Oh, but I know him." She looked up and smiled briefly. "He'll make a fuss to begin with—but in the end he'll come round. You see, he really does love me. It's only that when he came back unexpected ... well, there was the boy to think of. You can't pull kids into that kind of thing, can you? It seemed the best way out since he's off to sea so often. Only thing I'm really

71

glad about is that young Peter knows nothing about it. But I can't think where he was at the time."

"They came up from the boat at Southampton in a hired car. The chauffeur has told us that they dropped Peter at Paddington Station before they came on here."

"Oh, I see. Well, thank God for that. I wouldn't want the boy to think anything dirty about me."

Miss Lloyd said, "That's not the way to talk about it. You just got into a mess you couldn't properly handle. And you mustn't worry about the boy. He's got his father to look after him."

"But where have they gone? What will they do?"

"I'm sure you'll know all that in good time." She felt in her raincoat pocket, pulled out a wallet and took one of her cards from it. Handing it to the woman, she said, "That's my private address and phone number. You can usually get me early in the morning or late evening. If you want any help, or if there is anything I can do just give me a ring. Will you?"

"Oh, I will. And thank you. You've been so kind." Joan smiled suddenly. "Talking to you has already made me feel much better."

Before she turned to go, Miss Lloyd said, "Would you have any idea where they might have gone?"

"I don't know. Frank's car is still outside. Only place comes to my mind might be Ireland. All his wife's relations live there. Apart from them Frank didn't have anyone that I know of. Not kin that is."

*   *   *   *

The curtains of the flat's sitting room were undrawn. Mr. Rundell stood looking out at the evening traffic moving in the Park and up and down Bayswater Road. Cars, cars, cars, he thought; beady and bright-eyed monsters swallowing up the natural richness of trillions of years and spewing their effluent into the air for man to breathe. Perhaps in time evolution would take one of its freakish jumps and all humans would have adapted to breathing carbon monoxide—just as now

72

they drank with equanimity and no response from their taste buds their hundreds-of-times-recycled water. Perhaps in time, too, in the unlikely event of God rather than Satan prevailing, there would be no need of any of the thousands of kinds of organizations of the nature of the one which he served. Perhaps . . .

Over his shoulder, he said to Miss Lloyd, who was pouring the after-dinner coffee at the small table by the fireplace, "So what's your guess?"

"I don't know. I wish sometimes we didn't have to do quite so much guessing."

He laughed. "Just give me what you first thought when the poor woman spilled out her story. Put yourself in Courtney's place."

"I don't imagine he'd have done much thinking. He'd have gone to get the boy at Paddington. That's where he wrote the letter. On the hotel paper. He had two thousand pounds in his pocket. The boy's mad about trains. I think they'd have taken one."

"For where?"

"For Ireland? Fishguard to get a boat across?"

"To his first wife's people? Possibility. But not a strong one. You don't take your second wife's troubles back to the spring-time of love's first memories. But we'll cover it."

"Or he could have gone West . . . God knows, anywhere. One thing is certain though. You can't put out a call for them as though they were criminals."

"We can do it discreetly, though. No need for any *Wanted* notices outside police stations. Spread the quiet word around and it shouldn't take long. In fact, we've got to do it. The boy's walking around with the equivalent of dynamite on him."

"So we just put it quietly to the police?"

"Exactly. And there is no need for you to rush off. I have already done it. They'll pick them up in a few days at the most and keep an eye on them until we can get in touch with Courtney. He will give no trouble. Remember he still has two thousand pounds at stake for the boy when he does his little memory act. Now . . . shall we have some brandy with this coffee and then perhaps—though not too loudly—a little Beethoven?"

* * * *

As he heard the call tones at the end of the line, Tampion half turned and watched the traffic milling round Trafalgar Square and the evening crowd moving around the basins of the playing fountains, and Nelson on his column looking down on the moving wrack of humanity below. *England expects* ... Well, well, that was jolly O.K. if you were jolly well for good old England, but some there were who had turned privateers and if you ran a tight enough ship you had little to worry about except God's wrath. And you had that anyway, whatever you did or did not do. Funny about his father all those years ago wanting him to go in the Guards. Very odd, considering he was a Church of England parson as unwarlike as a tame rabbit...

A voice at the other end of the line broke in—"Grayson Insurance Company. Can I help you?"

Tampion said, "Stormbird here. The net's being spread for them. Nothing to do until I report again. O.K.?"

"Yes. Goodbye." The receiver was replaced at the end of the line.

Tampion left the box and began to walk towards his club in Pall Mall. A game of squash, a swim and then a leisurely dinner. Life was good and exciting so long as you kept your wits about you.

* * * *

They went down to Penzance on the train and found themselves bed and breakfast lodgings in the town, and began to take coach trips around the area. Their landlady was a good soul and did their laundry for them, and Courtney bought some extra socks and shirts for himself and the boy. There was nothing yet settled in his mind ... largely because at the moment he found himself unable to consider any future except

74

the coming day. He took only one positive move and that was to write to Mr Rundell because in common decency he felt he owed it to him. But he put no address on the letter. He took it, with Peter keeping him company, to the station and tipped the guard of a London train to post it at Paddington, saying that it was urgent. The guard looked a bit old-fashioned about doing it but agreed when Peter said, "You must have a lovely time— being on a train every day."

The guard, a West Country man, grinned and said, "Lovely is as lovely does, me dear. The train's all right but the trouble is some what rides on it."

The letter read:

> For personal reasons Peter and I have gone away on a trip for a while. I can't explain more than that and apologize to you for all this. But I have got to think things over and get them straight, especially this memory thing which I don't think now does the boy any good.

They took a coach trip that day to Land's End. In a few days May would be coming in and there was a growing warmth in the westerly wind that came sweeping over the cliffs. After lunch in the hotel he sat on a rock while Peter went off exploring this new territory. Gulls and other sea-birds wheeled and cried over the cliffs and the air was sweet with the new thyme blossom. Watching the birds, knowing little about them, he thought about Sarah. She had been a country girl, would have known the names of all the sea-birds and the cliff flowers, and had never been meant for London life ... had never been meant for a long life perhaps because God had loved her and taken her early ...

Peter came back to him, his hands full of flowers he had picked and a selection of empty snail shells, wind and rain burnished, lying in the palm of his hand like a collection of jewels, and said, "Can we buy a book that tells about flowers and birds and things, Dad?"

Courtney grinned, touched by the sparkle in Peter's eyes and the colour the fresh wind had brought to his cheeks. He said, "I thought you were only interested in trains."

75

"Course I'm not. That's when I'm in London. But now . . . well, it's no good being in the country and not learning about it, is it?"

"No, it isn't. We'll see what we can find in Penzance for you."

That evening when they were back at their lodgings and Peter had gone to bed, the landlady came into the sitting room and said, "Mr Courtney—could I have a few words with you?"

"Of course. What's the trouble?" And there was trouble, he could tell from her manner.

She said, "I don't know that there is. Not that I haven't had my share over the years. And that being so, I like to be fair to people, because trouble often sits on the wrong shoulders, and I'm no one for making judgments just on account of what other people say. You and your boy seem decent, nice folk."

"Well, I hope we are." He said it with a smile but unease was stirring in him. "Why don't you tell me what's on your mind?"

"I will because I believe in bein' straight and using my own judgment which is all in your favour—unless you tell me different. So I'll put a fair question to you. Have you and the boy done anything wrong? Anything that would have the police after you?"

"No, we haven't. So why don't you tell me the rest?"

She sat down on the arm of a settee and said, "I will—'cause I trust my own judgment and like to be fair to folks. You see, I went visiting this morning to a friend of mine who keeps a small hotel down the road. She likes a good old gossip, and for that matter, so do I. She said a plain-clothes policeman had been there a little earlier. He said he was checking hotels to see if he could find a Mr Courtney and his son from London. 'Course, she hadn't. But I have—and the point is sooner or later the police—when they've done the hotels in the town— will start on the lodging houses which means they'll come here. And not for the first time. So what's your answer to that?"

"It's quite simple. First, thank you very much for being so

76

straight with me. And secondly—the reason they might be looking for us is that my son and I went away for a trip together and when I came back unexpected I found my wife in bed with another man—"

"Never!"

"I'm afraid so. Luckily my son wasn't there. I'd dropped him off to play with some of his friends. I was so upset that I just walked out, picked him up, and took the first train to anywhere which turned out to be Penzance. And that's God's truth. I just suppose she's asked the police to find me." He knew, though, that it was not Joan, but almost certainly Mr Rundell who had done the asking.

She stood up. "Well, that's frank. And I'm sorry for you. So what are you going to do?"

"I just want to be left alone for a while with the boy, to think things over. Then I'll settle everything up."

"Well, in that case you'd better look for some other place to do your thinking, Mr Courtney. And sorry I am to say it—but it's for your own sake. When the police come I must tell them the truth of course."

"I would want you to. I don't want any trouble for you."

They took a coach—much to Peter's disgust—the next morning and went eastwards, back towards London but only as far as Tavistock just over the border from Cornwall into Devon where they found lodgings in a boarding house on the hill above the town on the road to Launceston and booked in under the name of Mr Grady and son, Peter.

He was, partly because he wanted to be, and also because he knew it was the wisest thing to do, almost entirely frank with Peter. It was one of the hardest things he had ever done in his life.

As they lay, each in his single bed, the window curtains drawn back to show the great wheel of the stars in the clear sky, and distantly now and then the call of owls coming from the valley below them, he said, "Are you awake, Peter?"

"Yes . . . why?"

"I want to tell you something. About why I came to find you at Paddington and why we went away like that. Didn't you find it a bit odd?"

"I suppose I did. But I didn't think about it much. Anyway, I liked it."

"That's good. I'm liking it too. Well ... perhaps you know from the other boys at school about people falling in love and getting married and how babies come along?"

"Oh, that. Yes, I know. But I don't like the way some of the boys go on."

"I'm glad you don't. It's a very private and a very special thing. You see, when I got home I found that Joannie had fallen in love with another man and didn't want me any more."

"What man?"

"Well ... your Uncle Chris. Only he isn't your uncle or Joannie's brother. That was all a pack of lies. So I just walked out and left them and came and found you. Do you understand?"

There was silence for a while and then Peter said calmly, "I never did think he was my uncle—only a pretend one. I mean Joannie pretending mostly. They used to kiss and cuddle one another when they didn't think I knew ... like when I'd come home from school a bit early and go round the back way to feed my rabbits what I used to have ... in the kitchen they would be."

"Why did you never tell me?"

"I don't know. I thought about that ... but I didn't know how to. And anyway I thought perhaps you knew and didn't mind." He paused for a while and then went on a little anxiously, "Do you really mean we're not going back to London ever?"

"Oh, some time. But not for a while. Not for some weeks."

"But what about the thing for Mr Rundell?"

Oh God, he thought, what do I say? The truth about Joan had run off his back like water from a duck's, thank God. How on earth was he to handle the Rundell affair? He realized at once that there was no question here of telling the truth. How could he, anyway? What he guessed for himself was one thing. Once he had known of the Comte de Servais' death, and added

78

to that Miss Lloyd's sudden rush to get them out of the country as soon as possible, there had been no escaping the fact that something of great importance to them was now locked up in his boy's mind. And if it was all that important it could mean danger for the boy. He felt sick and suddenly old and weary because he had half-known or half-guessed this from the start and yet had gone through with it. To give himself time, he asked, "Do you remember anything of what the Comte de Servais said to you?"

Peter laughed. "Oh, yes. He said his real name was Alphonse Grubais and when he was at school in England he was called All Grubby. I thought that was funny."

"No. I mean when you did your memory thing with him?"

"No, I don't. You know I never do—except that it was in French to start with. Did it have anything to do with Joannie?"

"No, of course not. Well, anyway I've told you about Joannie and because I don't want her to find us yet—and she might ask the police to try and do that—I thought we ought to change our name. So when we came here today I told the land- lady that I was Mr Grady and you were Peter Grady, naturally."

"Why didn't you say O'Grady? That's what mother was called before she married you."

"I didn't think of that. But, anyway, you're now Peter Grady. How does it sound?"

"Oh, not bad. Peter Grady. I bet I forget now and then."

"Well, just try to remember."

"All right. Are we going to be away long?"

"I don't know how long. We'll just have to see."

"Well, if it's going to be long—we should find somewhere proper to live. By ourselves, I mean."

"Why?"

"Well, if Joannie asks the police to find us they'd tell all the police stations to look out for us. All over the country—and they always check up on hotels and boarding houses. I know that because May said she had a brother who worked in a garage and he ran off with the takings one week and he went on a spree staying at hotels and he used to sign in with his own name—and they got him even before he'd spent all the money."

"That wasn't very bright of him."

"No. May said he was as thick as two boards and he finished up in prison."

Courtney laughed. "Well, that's not something that could happen to us. Now off to sleep with you and we'll think about finding a place of our own."

"That would be nice."

Lying there, it was not long before he heard the boy's breathing tones change and knew that he was asleep. Although he was no stranger to it from Peter, it never ceased to amaze him how unexpectedly composed and knowledgeable the young were these days. And how instinctively careful not to involve themselves in the private affairs of their grown-ups. Peter had known that something was going on between Joan and Chris, but had said nothing. Grown-ups lived in another world and the wisest thing to do was not to get mixed up with them. Young eyes and ears were sharp—but so was their instinct to avoid involvement or upsetting the status quo. And they had a simple wisdom that took them straight to the core of a problem. Not just change your name and yet go on living in boarding houses and hotels. Find a hole, a burrow—and not in any populated warren, either. Somewhere away on your own . . . He had got to have time to work things out. Grubais had been murdered, but he had passed something to Peter. For the first time he began to see clearly the menace which over-shadowed them. The Comte de Servais' murder gave another dimension to the problem for it meant that other people than those that Rundell served were active and would want what-ever had been passed to the boy never to be released. They would want Peter . . . Oh, Christ! He groaned slightly to himself. It was all too much, just too bloody much for him. And that damned Rundell, so damned nice to the boy, and then afterwards over the brandy dragging him—and by God, not unwilling with the money dangling like a carrot before him—into all this dangerous mess. Holy Jesus . . . if Sarah were looking down now and by miracle could make it she would stand square to him and spit in his face with deserved contempt.

*　　*　　*　　*

Peter woke early in his strange bed. His father was still asleep. Sparrows were quarrelling under the eaves outside his window. Now and again cars passed up and down the hill. Across the patch of blue sky he could see a jet tracing a white trail of vapour. Scratching the blue belly of the skies, his mother used to say, as though they wanted to get through to heaven when all the time it was right here down on earth and needed only the taking if you had hands clean enough to pick it up. Funny, nice things like that she used to say. And she never got fussed up about things like his father did. Poor Dad, he really did get fussed up sometimes. His mother often said straight to his face while he, himself, was in the room—'Frank Courtney—you're your own worst enemy. Before you come to a corner you see trouble around it. What you don't understand, me darling, is that trouble would never bother to hide to trip you up because you're always ready to oblige by doing it yourself before you get to the corner.' Other things she said, too; and some of them so saucy they made you laugh. Joan was nice, no matter about all that Chris stuff. Warm and comfortable—but she was absolutely daft and thought that she could bamboozle you. Like when he had—though he would never tell his father this—come down in stockinged feet from his bedroom one evening, while Dad was out, to get his book he'd left there and found the two of them standing up with their arms around one another kissing and she tried to pretend that Uncle Chris was showing her a new dance step. Without music, too. Oh, she was all right. But his mother. He knew what she would have said. 'When people's kissing, youngsters should be missing.' But that was always with Dad. They'd always been at it.

And now, poor old Dad. There wasn't really anything to fuss about. He'd got upset about Joannie and left her. But there wasn't any need for all this changing of names. He'd done nothing wrong. If he didn't want to go back, he didn't have to. But if that was how he felt ... well, it was all a bit of fun, changing names and wanting to find somewhere to live for a while before they went back. He wasn't against it. Nor would half the chaps in the school have been either. Peter Grady? Well, it wasn't too bad a name. If he was that much older he could wear a false moustache ... he wriggled in the bed with silent laughter. But when it had passed, he thought solemnly ... well, we'll have to do something about it. Shops were the place. Newsagents. Like the one in Praed Street. Always had notices pinned up about flats and rooms to let. And sometimes the funny ones that the coloured boys put up for a joke—when the shopkeeper wasn't looking. *Young lady with three legs wants to meet desirable gent with one for ballroom dancing.* And—*Will swop my lovely missus for good guitar. Trial period both sides if desired.*

From the other side of the room, his father yawned and said, "What are you giggling about?"

"Something I just thought about. Are we going to look for somewhere to live today?"

"Why not—today's better than tomorrow because—"

"Tomorrow never comes."

They both laughed.

CHAPTER SIX

THE MINISTER HAD an illuminated tropical fish tank in his room and as he talked Rundell watched the aimless movement of its inhabitants, pleasantly isolated in their little world, fed, and warmed, and serviced and perhaps secure in the knowledge that there was no other universe than the one they inhabited. Maybe their world was no different in essence from his own. They loved and quarrelled, took likes and dislikes . . . perhaps complained in their own way about the food and the slightest change in temperature from their known and comfortable norm. And, no doubt, among them were the killers and the victims, and the inevitable insistence on status. Don't come too close to my corner, my sheltering frond of weed.

He said, "They were in Penzance—that is a matter of fact. I also had a letter from the father—posted in London—on the day the police discovered they had been in Penzance, but had left that morning. The postmark was Paddington so the father probably got some railway employee to post it for him. He's developed a conscience about the way the boy was to be used."

"How could he know about that?"

"Well—two thousand pounds down—and two thousand waiting for the boy. That's not normal. He knew that right from the start. And he could have read the papers since. De Servais' murder was carried in the papers over here. On top of everything, too, he came back to find his wife in bed with another man. We've checked his bookshop. He's got a part-time man in who has now taken it over. He had a letter from Courtney, too."

"What's your big worry?" The Minister smiled. "Or am I misreading you?"

"No, you're not, Minister. What happened to the Count could happen to the boy if *they* ever came to know that de Servais' death came too late to protect them."

"Innocent blood on your hands?"

"Yes."

"And not for the first time. That's the perennial hazard of your work, and through you mine." The Minister spread his well-manicured fingers and examined them. Then with a shrug, he went on, "Well, the sooner you find the boy and debrief him the sooner we shall both sleep somewhat sounder at night. You could make the search public ... radio, television, with some bland cover story."

"And give aid to the other side, possibly? You know what I'm talking about, Minister."

"Of course. They won't wait to get the list out of the boy. The best kept secrets are those buried deep. And I'm sure you don't want me to transfer the whole business to another section. That would just double the risk. So—God help us—there is nothing to be done except to keep praying and find him fast. How much do you trust Miss Lloyd and Tampion and, of course, me?"

Rundell shrugged his shoulders. "Implicitly—until I'm proved wrong and that moment not too late a one to safeguard our interests and the boy's life."

"In that order?"

"There can be no other."

"Well, there it is, and ironically the whole thing started because one lovely woman stooped to folly. Which, of course, is a perennial possibility in this world."

*   *   *   *

While his father was inside the tobacconist's shop getting cigarettes and a paper, Peter waited outside and began to read the notices on a small board hanging in the entrance to the shop. His father had walked right by it without noticing it. He was like that, he thought. When his head was full of problems his eyes seemed to go blank.

There were a lot of prams for sale and a piebald pony "suitable for a beginner". He ran his eyes down the collection of business cards ... chiropodists and secretarial schools, lawn mowers serviced ... several secondhand cars for sale, a vacuum cleaner, *as new, twenty-five pounds o.n.o.,* and, *Let lady, Cordon bleu trained, take over your party and anniversary functions—estimates free.* And one, with some faint echo of Praed Street in it. *Young man seeks companionship opp. sex. Interests, music, bird watching, and country pursuits. Own car.* And another—*Why be shy, lonely? Exploit your hidden personality. Join our Friendship Club.* Then followed a telephone number which he did not read because his eye was caught by a postcard reading—*Fully equipped caravan to let. Isolated, idyllic situation. Far from the madding crowd. Apply—Hawkpitch Cottage, Sleadon, near Launceston.*

His father coming out of the shop at this moment, he pointed out the notice to him, and said, "Why don't we go and look at it, Dad? We could live there and nobody would bother us. No landladies. What do you think?"

"Um ... I don't know."

"Oh, come on, Dad. We could look at it, anyway. And it doesn't sound the kind of place the police would come nosing around."

Courtney hesitated for a moment or two and then smiled. "All right. But we would have to do all our own cooking. And I'm hopeless you know."

"Oh, we can manage that. Besides we don't have to cook much."

"Well, we could look at it. Where is it, I wonder?"

"Why don't you go back in and buy a map? Don't ask the chap because if the police came to him he might remember about it. We'll find it on our own, and if we like it and it's still free we could move up there tomorrow."

As his father went back into the shop, Peter sighed a little to himself. Something seemed to have come over his father in the last days. He usually was all up and go, but now he was sort of drifty and moony ... well, he supposed the Joannie thing was a bit of a shock. Grown-ups always made a big fuss of their

85

troubles. But what was the point if you could do nothing about them? Like May at Paddington had once said, "I'm gone past taking notice of troubles. You give 'em houseroom and you soon find yourself on the street. Pretend they ain't there and you keep a roof over your head—and if that falls, well ... there's an end to all your troubles."

When his father came out of the shop they went to a café and studied the map. They soon found Launceston which was not very far from Tavistock and—so the waitress told them when asked—was on a bus route. Then Peter found Sleadon which was, from the look of it on the map, no more than a few houses grouped near a bridge over a river called the Tamar.

They took the bus to Launceston, but on the advice of the driver they got off some way before they reached it and took a side road, signposted Sleadon, which led down the hill to the river. Hawkpitch Cottage was the first of the four cottages which made up Sleadon.

A comfortable looking country woman came to the door, wiping her floury hands on the apron round her ample waist and, after they had explained their business, said warmly, "Well, me dears, if you'll wait a bit I'll give a ring and see if her Ladyship can see you. I do knows of course that the caravan's empty. Most always is. It's a dampy old place up there."

She went back into her cottage and Courtney said, "That doesn't sound very promising, does it?"

"Oh, they always say things like that, Dad." As he spoke Peter was far from sure that *they* did, but he felt in some way that just for the time being he had to keep his father happy and up to the mark. It was funny, he thought, how sometimes grown-ups got into a gloomy state and fussed over every small thing, making trouble for themselves before they even started. Like Joannie when she put a Yorkshire pudding in the oven always saying—*"I know it won't rise proper. They never do for me."* He had said to her one day—*"You know why they don't, don't you? It's because the pudding hears you say it and right away loses heart and doesn't try."* And now here was his father slipping into the same way. Which wasn't like him. It had all started since he had met that Mr Rundell and they had gone to France. At that moment

86

for the first time a disturbing question floated into his
1. Had his father and Mr Rundell—and perhaps Miss
d—between them done something wrong? And all that
about Joannie and Chris was just made up? Well,
vay, he could see that whatever it was, it was up to him at
noment to keep the party cheerful.

'hen the woman came back she said, "Her Ladyship says
1 meet you up there in an hour. But don't set no great store
hat—she's no great one for keeping to time. Here's the key
e caravan."

s his father took the key, Peter asked, "Who's her Lady-
, ma'am?"

he woman laughed. "She's Lady Diana Stormont. Her
ly used to own most of the land around here once. But not
. Come down in the world, they have. Not that you would
s it from the way she acts. But don't mind her bark—it's
no bite to it unless you really cross her. Now, let me tell you
way to get up there . . ."

he told them, and following her instructions they went
n the road a piece and found the entrance to an old, over-
vn driveway that wound uphill through a great standing of
ent oaks and a wild confusion of overgrown rhododendron
les. To one side of the driveway a stream came tumbling
falling over small rock falls, and swirling round deep pools
hung with growths of ferns. At the top of the wood, the
and lost its steepness and the driveway curled across a
gh patch of neglected meadow land on which a few bull-
grazed. Seeing them, the bullocks, in the way of their
l, galloped towards them, kicking up their heels, and ac-
panied them to a far gate with a stone style at its side, over
ch they both climbed quickly, grateful to be free of the
sts. A few minutes later they were in a small clearing on the
e of a stand of well-grown larches and firs. Below them the
l fell away to the distant river with thickly wooded slopes
ond it. On the edge of the clearing, at the side of the now
owed stream, stood the caravan. .

: was a big caravan jacked up on sturdy brick pillars, its
els gone as though, once brought here, it was evident they

would never be used again. Curtains were drawn over
windows. There were two dustbins tucked away in a s
lean-to on the edge of the clearing, and close to them a very
flagpole, its halyards, cleated home at the bottom, maki
gentle slapping sound against the mast as the fresh br
worked and fretted at them. In the front of the caravan,
piece of level grass, was a long, roughly fashioned table wi
bench on each side of it.

Peter said, "It'll be fun having our meals out here."

His father laughed. "Just so long as there's no v
blowing—otherwise we'd take off and finish in the river d
there."

"But don't you like it, Dad? I think it's super."

"For a couple of mountain goats, yes."

"Oh, Dad. . . ."

Courtney grinned. "No, it's fine. Just what we want.
the advertisement said—Far from the madding crowd. B
didn't mention the madding bullocks and the moun
climb." Then, turning his face away from his son, and loo
away across the valley, he thought—What the devil are
doing up here? How did it all happen? Suddenly the wor
our world—has gone topsy-turvey and we're like a coupl
gypsies, living from day to day. And then the thought
denly hit him, bringing a choke to his throat . . . If it had
been different. If it had all been taking place in some dre
land of lost happiness, and he were here now with Sarah
the boy . . . just holidaying. She would have loved it, it was
style, and so would have been his. And he could fancy
saying, "Aaaaah, be Jasus (putting on her Irish to make P
laugh) and what could be finer now than livin' almost chee
cheek with the angels and the whole world at your feet, and
Devil a thousand miles away on his dirty business, too ha
workin' the dirty cratur, to give a mind to us?" And then s
denly, the partly disturbing, partly warming fancy struck
that she was here, unseen, but guarding and that it was
working through Peter, that had brought them here. In
moment he was gripped by a devastating surge of self-p
Jesus Christ—how had all this happened?

At this moment Peter said, "Somebody's coming."

And somebody was. Away to their right where the driveway ran straight and level along the fringe of the plantation there came the sound of a bicycle bell ringing. A few moments later Lady Diana Stormont came into view, riding an old bicycle, keeping unsteadily to the crown of the worn drive to avoid the ruts on either side.

She came into the caravan clearing, dismounted, and let the machine drop to the ground. She walked towards them smiling, taking from her head a man's cap which she dropped on the picnic table, and gave her head a shake to free her pale, almost ash-blond hair, and Peter thought she was the most beautiful lady he had ever seen . . . well, excepting his mother. But different. Her eyes were blue and she had a way of flicking her eyelids as though she were trying to say something to you with some special signalling. She wasn't young, though. Almost as old as his dad, at least. But there was something about her that said *special*—but she was dressed something awful. Muddy old gumboots with her blue dungaree bottoms tucked into them, and a khaki shirt with the sleeves rolled up over sun-browned arms and, close about her neck, a little gold chain from which, just showing in the opening of her shirt, hung a gold crucifix. He couldn't believe that she was a lady, and an honourable one—whatever that meant.

She came up to them and said brightly, "Mr Grady and son. Looking flushed and hot from a long climb. Never mind. If you stay—and I must say, from a first glance, I'm inclined in your favour—you'll think nothing of it." Then to his father, she said, "Have you looked over the caravan?"

Courtney said, "Not yet, my Lady. We were just getting our breath back. This is my son, Peter. And I'm Frank Grady. We're on a sort of holiday."

"Aye, that's this country's disease. Everyone's on a sort of a holiday. But let's not spoil a lovely day with a consideration of the country's problems. Now then—let me show you round. But I must say this first—if you decide for it, then it's a deposit of the first month's rent in advance. The world is full of rogues and I've had a few up here. One week—which is all they ever intended—and they go, kissing the back of their hand to you as their only payment."

Courtney said, "Don't worry. I'll pay in advance. We're on holiday for a few weeks. We come from London."

"And a good place to come from. Though I must say, when I was that much younger I thought it was Jerusalem the golden. Now first of all, I can tell you—the water in the stream is good to drink. God sent it. Not some damned purification plant." She looked at Peter and grinned. "Mind you—there'll be the odd tadpole this time of the year. Just pretend nothing's happened and put it on the side of your plate politely. And anything you want in the way of groceries and so on—just give Mrs Preston at Hawkpitch a list and she'll get it for you when the grocery van calls."

She took the key which his father was holding and opened the caravan door. She led them through it, explaining things and opening drawers and cupboards to show them where things were.

She said, "All the blankets and cutlery stuff are at my place. Leave anything around here and someone will thank you for it and you'll see it no more. If you take it I'll have it in here when you say. The charge is ten pounds a week. That's forty pounds in advance for the month. And be nice to Mrs Preston and she'll do anything for you. Cross her and she'll put a curse on you which you'll be long in shaking off. She used to be my nurse in the old days at the big house across the river. Now it's a nursing home for the rich who can afford any ailment they fancy. *Sic transit gloria mundi*. Translate, Peter."

Surprised, Peter was silent for a moment and then managed, grappling with his school Latin, "Thus travels the glory of the world."

"Not bad." She turned and picked up a roll of cloth from the top of the closed kitchen sink. "And this is the house flag. Hoist it at daybreak and strike it at sunset. And if you're ever in trouble drop it to half-mast and the whole county will come charging up here to help you—perhaps." She winked at Peter and he laughed out loud, liking her a lot, but he could tell that his father was a long way from making up his mind about her yet. But then he always was with new people.

Peter said, "What is the flag, ma'am?"

"It's our family flag. The Stormont arms. I won't trouble you with the heraldic description. When you fly it you'll see for yourself. Well now, Mr Grady—what do you think of it? Do you want it?"

Peter saw the hesitation in his father. Anything new and he liked time to think about it. But this time the hesitation was brief, almost non-existent. He said, "I think it will suit us fine."

"Good. And when will you move in?"

"Tomorrow morning, won't we, Dad?" said Peter.

Lady Diana laughed. "That's what I like about the young these days. Before you've time to open your mouth there they are speaking up for you."

Peter's father laughed, and said, "We like it—and we want it. Shall I pay now for the month?"

"No, tomorrow will do when you're in residence. So, there we are, all settled. Now I must dash off. I've got to milk Alice. She's the family cow, and like all Jerseys she's fussy about times. Keep her waiting an hour and you'll only get half the milk you expect. Goodbye then."

When she was gone Peter's father sat down on one of the side seats which opened to make a bed, took a big breath and said, "Did we just have a visit—or was it a sudden gust of wind blowing through?"

Peter laughed, and was happy because he could sense that his father was in good humour. He said, "I liked her. But I bet she could give the rough side of her tongue if you crossed her."

"What woman can't? However . . . you like it? You're all for it?"

"I am. Aren't you?"

"Yes, I am."

Peter picked up the rolled flag and shook its folds free and spread it on the table. On a blue background there were two rearing, golden stags looking as though they were fighting one another while over their heads, wings wide spread hovered some kind of eagle. Underneath the crest were the words—

Nosce Teipsum.

Peter asked, "What's that mean, Dad?"

His father shook his head. "Search me. You'll have to ask Lady Diana sometime. Come on—let's get back and tell our good landlady we're leaving."

*   *   *   *

Two days later Teddy Tampion came into Mr Rundell's room and put a memorandum in front of him, saying, "This just came through."

Rundell picked it up and read it. It was a message which had come from the Tavistock police saying that in the course of checking all boarding houses they had found one in which a Mr Frank Grady and his son, Peter, had been staying until the day before the check was made. They fitted the description of the father and son Courtney. The landlady had said they had left the morning before the police called and she had no idea where they were going.

Rundell pushed the minute from him and said, "That's helpful, isn't it? They could be a hundred miles away by now. Anyway, you'd better spread the word that they may well now be using the Grady name. Wonder why they picked that name?"

Tampion said, "That was his first wife's maiden name. Almost. She was an O'Grady. Maybe that's where the boy got his gift. A touch of the Irish magic. One thing it tells us for sure, though, is that Courtney isn't anxious to be found and knows or guesses that we are looking for him. What's to be done?"

"Nothing. Just let the police go beavering on, but notify all of them that they are now using the name Grady. We don't want any big song and dance about this."

Back in his own room Tampion, drawing with some skill a family of owls sitting wide-eyed on a branch with a full moon in the background, thought to himself that the police could go beavering on as much as they liked but he, himself, had doubts as to whether that would lead to Frank Courtney. A change of

92

name meant that the man in some way either knew, or had reason to guess, that a search was on for him and the boy. He'd be a fool not to because he must have known from the start that Rundell hadn't just sent him to France on a joy ride. The money on the table between them would have made that plain. And he was sensible enough to know that being badgered from pillar to post by the police would soon end in his capture. Man's instincts were still primitive enough to send him to ground when the chase hotted up. And Rundell, dear old Easy Rundell, wouldn't be caring a damn about the boy unless it were a known fact to him that the Count had been able to pass his message before he was killed. Not that he, himself, would be so worried about that if he could have known that his own name was not on the list. De Servais the mystery man . . . no one ever knowing quite which side he was on. And at the end probably tired of the whole damned business, getting a load of mischief off his chest, and not caring whether he lived or died. Well, he himself cared whether *he* lived. Life was sweet, brother. The wind on the heath and the bubbles in the champagne, the sharp chill of risk that did more for the senses than wine, women or song.

On his way home that evening he put a call through to the Grayson Insurance Company. At the end of his talk he said, "And above all, he's got to be a countryman and not stand out like a canary in a flock of jolly old starlings."

*　　　*　　　*　　　*

Peter had lain awake for a long time on their first night in the caravan. In London there were always familiar noises, no matter what time of night it was—the sound of cars, people coming from parties, noisy and laughing as they went up the street, distant clocks striking and the drone overhead of air traffic. But around the caravan there was . . . well, not exactly silence, but different noises which it took him some time to place. The halyards on the flagpole made a gentle *tap, tap, tap* in the slightest breeze. And now he knew the sudden screech of an owl and could pick out distantly the barking of farm dogs

... one far down the hill at Sleadon and another one over towards where Lady Diana lived. As noises they were all right but not as comforting as the London noises. He didn't think that really he would care to live in the country for good—but until Dad got things sorted out he didn't mind.

They had moved in the day after they had first seen the caravan and Lady Diana had come over in a muddy old Land Rover with their sheets and blankets and she had shown him how to cleat the flag to the halyard and haul it to the top of the mast and break it out. He had asked her what *Nosce Teipsum* meant and she had said, "Know thyself". That didn't make much sense to him. Surely everyone knew themselves? Pretty poor lookout if they didn't. Though, come to think of it, it was odd how you could find out that you didn't know other people—people close to you—as well as you thought. His Dad, now. He was always such a one for getting things organized at home. *We're going there. We're going to do this at such and such a time. Wear your best suit. No need to dress up. And afterwards we'll go to this and see that ...* Everything pat. But not now. He just mooned around and let him cook their eggs and bacon and make the coffee. Though he did do the washing up. However, he didn't mind. He was enjoying himself. Tomorrow Mrs Preston's husband was going to bring up the groceries they had ordered. He was a gamekeeper or something like that. And Lady Diana had been pulling his leg about the tadpoles in the water. There weren't any. It was as clear as crystal. *Know thyself ...* that was a kind of daft motto. You couldn't help knowing yourself. Though knowing other people was different. You couldn't always know them. Like Joannie and Chris. They were both nice people—so why could they have done what they did to Dad? He really was still very upset about it. Still, all that would pass. That's what old Blackie Timms said—*Sun goes down and sun comes up, boy. And nothin' changes. Each day you got to live with your same old self and the same old other folk droppin' their litter all around.*

Outside there was a rattle and scraping at the dustbin behind the caravan. He knew what that was because Lady Diana had told them. "There's an old dog fox up here, and

94

when he goes courting, which he does at this time of year, he calls in and has a look in the bin for scraps."

Peter—used to night noises now—yawned and turned over and slept.

*　　*　　*　　*

Albert Ainsley Horsfell booked into the Royal Hotel, Tavistock, and the first evening there, chatting at the bar over a drink before dinner, a chubby, cheerful-looking middle-aged man in old-fashioned kneebreeches and a well-kept suede jacket, let it be known that he was on holiday and a keen birdwatcher, fingering absently his Royal Society for the Protection of Birds tie. Vaguely, for he had an arcane sense of humour, he wondered what the rather washed-out blonde woman serving him would have thought had he said— "Actually, of course, dearie, I'm down here to knock off some snotty-nosed boy—if I can find him. Got a handy little rifle in a case under the back seat of my Renault 14. Breaks down easily. Just a twist of a coin and the barrel and action can be removed for easy packing. Nice French walnut stock and I can knock a blue-bottle off a cow pat at a hundred yards." In fact he knew what she would say because she was the kind who only stood and served and seldom listened because she was so full of her own gab and troubles—"Well, fancy that, love. And as I was saying, this feller comes in ..."

People, he thought, were too full of their own troubles and woes and boring pleasantries. He went into dinner, taking with him a sheaf of house agents' particulars of furnished cottages to let in the district. Had to be furnished. Do for themselves. Away from the nosiness of neighbours. Tucked away. Some sylvan retreat. If they were here he would find them. Take the boy in his sights and then—*wham*—to start the heavenly choir of angels at their singing to welcome another little innocent in.

He ate a prawn cocktail, smothered with indifferent mayonnaise, an overcooked fillet steak with tinned carrots and soggy mashed potatoes and topped it off with a factory-made slice of

95

apple pie whose pastry looked and tasted like soggy brown paper. He thoroughly enjoyed the meal because he paid no attention to it. He was no one for finicky details when he was enjoying himself. But work now . . . ah, then nothing was overlooked, condoned or forgiven. Only the highest standard was accepted. And it was, of course, doubly pleasant to mix work with pleasure for he had long eschewed the droll, misshapen passions of most men. Birds were his delight. He knew a hawk from a handsaw . . . heron, of course, as anyone would know . . . and a sedge warbler from a reed warbler. Yes, he was really looking forward to this assignment. No rush. And no matter if the boy wasn't down here. He would get his money just the same—though, sadly, not the bonus for putting the whipping on top of the fruit salad. Long ago and far away he had been a boy—and a bloody awful time he had had of it, too. Mother religion mad and a father who was one of Nature's born sadists. Both dead—but how his father went. . . . Ah, that would be telling.

*　　　*　　　*　　　*

Bert Preston was having his high tea at six o'clock. He was a short-set, solidly built man with a round, weather-beaten face. He was a man of fifty, not much given to talk unless he had taken a few more pints of cider than was his wont, and even then he could talk more sense than would be expected.

His wife, putting steak and kidney pudding and garden greens in front of him, said, "You dropped all that stuff off for them up at the caravan today, did 'ee?"

"Aye."

"Well, not quite Bert Preston. You forgot to take the paraffin for their lamps. They'll be sitting in the dark up there."

"Damn—well I'm goin' up that way later. I'll take it then. The fish be runnin' and we're overdue a visit from poachers. Lordship's days there was a bailiff and three unders to look after things. Now the syndicate won't go to more than me, and look old-fashioned when the night boys clear a couple of their pools. Worth it, too—with the price of salmon these days.

Small risks—big profits. Lordship's day they would have had their arses peppered with shot and be put away. Now—these syndicate gents expect one man to do miracles. I wonder Her Ladyship can bear to live up there at the old farm and see everything turning topsy-turvy. Who be these two then? Londoners?"

"Reckon so."

"Seem decent enough, first sight. But you never can tell. Aye, not even with the syndicate gentlemen. Some not above puttin' a shrimp on to take a fish, or knockin' down a hen at a cocks-only shoot. Where's Judy?"

"It's youth club night in Launceston. She's cycled over."

"I'll tan her arse if she's not back by eleven."

"Aye—that's what you say when she isn't around. But one smile from her and she's got you round her little finger."

He grinned. "Well, it were the same way with you, mother—and you took advantage of it."

After his supper he drove up the old driveway to the caravan through the growing dusk and found the man and the boy sitting in the caravan by candle-light. He apologized for having forgotten the oil that morning, and filled their two oil lamps for them and trimmed the wicks.

As he left, the boy—a nice enough youngster—walked with him to his car and said, "It's a rough ride all up here, isn't it, Mr Preston?"

"Aye—" he grinned, "—but my bottom's got well used to it. You from London?"

"Yes."

"You like it here?"

"In some ways."

"Well—there's one difference that's good. You'll never be knocked down by a bus here. You ever done any shooting or fishing?"

"No shooting. But I fished once or twice with my grandfather in Ireland. On a lough for trout. I didn't get anything, though." He grinned. "Grandfather said it was because I put the worm on upside down."

Preston chuckled. "Well, perhaps if you stay long enough,

97

I'll take you fishing one day—maybe for something a bit bigger than a trout."

As he drove off into the fast-growing dark Bert Preston shook his head. A daughter was fine and he had no grumbles—though in a couple of years when the lads got after her he could see he might—but a son was what a man needed. Someone to carry on where you left off. That was the trouble here ... his Lordship going and after him, first his wife, then three fine sons, one in the Navy and two in the Air Force, all wiped out, and now only Lady Diana left, and everything having to be sold up and the shooting and fishing syndicated and she left sitting over at Hightop Farm with a few acres and a cow and a rough old bit of hillside and moor pasture. Wouldn't even let the Forestry Commission take it over and plant it proper for her. Stubborn. Like her father, like her brothers—but no real head for money. Not a one of them. The folk who knew about that were the jumped-up Jimmies and Janies who stayed over the river at the luxury hotel which had once been the family home. Though you had to say that they kept it all in better shape over there than ever his Lordship did.

*　　　*　　　*　　　*

Albert Horsfell was a methodical man. He bought a large-scale map of Tavistock and district and drew a circle with a radius of ten miles around it. He divided the circle into quadrants and tossed a coin—after all the Gods of chance sometimes helped—as to which one he should pick first. He then proceeded to go over his chosen ground, following a precise routine. First he checked all the houses and cottages to let furnished which he had obtained from two or three local agents. He knew perfectly well that, in theory, the fact that they had given him the particulars of these places should mean that they were unoccupied. But any man who expects efficiency from house agents, he considered, was a simpleton wandering in an Alice-in-Wonderland world. In the first quadrant he chose he found two out of the five houses given to him already had occupants. Having exhausted his estate-agent list in a

98

quadrant, he visited all the village post offices and stores to see if they carried notices of places to let furnished. Father and son would not be lugging furniture around with them. People who put up notices in shops could easily forget to take them down. Once the money was coming in, who had a thought for a badly scrawled postcard?

Then came the public houses, the hotels, and anyone he could engage in talk. "Looking for some friends of mine. Said they were going to rent a holiday place around here. Father and son—boy's about thirteen. Nice kid. Grady's the name. Like a damned fool I've lost the address." Wearisome work, but then if he were lucky the pay in the end would be good. And, anyway, when he really got bored he could always sit on some stream bank and do a little quiet bird-watching. All work and no play... And the weather was keeping fine, so that it was good to feel the sun on him, and high spring was bursting out all over so that not only young men's fancies, but the fancies of all things in creation, were turning to thoughts of love and mating. Not that love figured in his life much—and then only commercially and transiently. His mother and father had put him off marriage, the stars be thanked. Better to marry than to burn. Don't you believe it, Albert Horsfell.

Every evening from a public call box he telephoned a report to the London number which had been given him. After that he listened to the barmaid at the hotel for a while, then ate his dinner with relish whatever it was and often he couldn't remember by the time he went to bed where he sat up, propped by his pillows, and wrote up his nature log.

He had started his search in the north-east quadrant of his circle and was working round anti-clockwise, and sometimes it took him two or more days to cover a quadrant thoroughly. The caravan lay in the north-west quadrant.

CHAPTER SEVEN

SOMETIMES IN THE mornings Peter would walk up to Hightop Farm to get their daily milk, leaving his father to tidy up the caravan. His father was more his old self now—cheerful, not moping around, and even beginning to get fussy about keeping the caravan and its site tidy. Just like he had once been in the bookshop. Everything in its place, and a place for everything. Not that you could say that, though, for Hightop Farm. It wasn't exactly dirty, but nothing seemed to be in its right place. Books on chairs, gum boots under the kitchen table and fishing rods and tackle heaped in a corner, and if you didn't look out you'd find yourself stepping into a saucer of cat's milk or the dog's bowl because there was no set place for them to be. Lady Diana called the cats and when they came she put the milk down wherever she happened to be. Same with the dog, and there was a pile of magazines and papers in one corner which was always falling over. He hadn't seen any of the rest of the house, but he wondered if it were the same. It wouldn't have suited Joannie. She was a demon for dusting and everything in its place.

He knew his way around by now outside. There was a small, weedy patch of vegetable garden and a little fenced-in paddock where the house cow, a pony, and two goats lived. Down the hill slope a little was a biggish pond with a small island in the middle where a few ducks lived to be safe from foxes.

One morning Lady Diana said to him, "Are you beginning to feel better since you've been up here?"

"Better, ma'am?"

"Yes. Your father said he'd brought you down to get some colour in your cheeks. Though I must say you never looked exactly ailing to me, boy."

Peter laughed. "I feel fine. Always have."

Lady Diana said with a smile, "You mean your father wasn't being exactly truthful with me? What have you two been up to? Robbed a bank?"

"Some hope."

"What then?" She sat down across the kitchen table facing him where he was perched opposite her on a stool with the glass of milk and piece of cake before him which she had given him. "Or is it too private to tell me?"

He could have said that it was, but he had the feeling that she wouldn't let it go at that. Women were like that. But he knew that he couldn't tell her about Joannie. That would upset his father, and he didn't want that to happen now that he was getting cheerful again.

He said, "Well, if I tell you you won't tell my father I told you, will you?"

She smiled. "Between us. I swear."

"Well, it was because of this memory thing of mine. I went round doing it a lot because it pleased Dad and he made some money out of it. Not that I think he needed it because he's got this bookshop in London which is being looked after by a friend of his now. And then I went to France and did it. And, I don't know, but Dad seemed to be all upset about it afterwards. So when we got back he said we'd go off and have a holiday and forget all about it, and I wouldn't have to do it any more."

She was confused and suspected that probably she was not getting the full truth, that in some way she had, without intent, embarrassed Peter and put him in an awkward position which was the last thing she had intended. But when you lived alone so damned much you found that loneliness, and living in the past, wore away your natural and decent sense of discretion. If she didn't watch it she would finish up as some bad-tempered old gossip. She gave him a warm smile, and said, "Well, that's all very clear. But what do you mean your memory thing? But don't tell me if it's a secret."

Peter laughed, relieved that he wouldn't have to go into any talk about Joannie, and said, "Oh, it's a thing I do. About remembering. You see it's like this ..."

He went on and explained his gift to her. When he finished she said, "Well, I never heard of anything like that before in my life." She laughed. "I've got a head like a sieve. I could never remember poetry. And you can do it in French?"

"Yes. That's what I did in France. But you won't tell my father I told you, will you? Now it's all finished he doesn't want people to know."

"Of course I won't. But I'm glad you told me. And your mother's in London, looking after the house while you two enjoy yourselves?"

"Yes. But she's my stepmother. My mother was Irish. She died some years ago, but I still miss her a lot, and so does Dad I know. But Joannie's very nice." He paused for a moment and she caught the momentary tightening of his lips and a quick, nervous blink of his eyes, and knew what was in him, and felt shame in herself for having, even without intent, brought him to this point.

"I'm sure she is. And so are you. I'll tell you a secret. You're the nicest boy that's ever been in the caravan."

"Oh, I don't believe that. You're just blarneying me."

"Cross my heart, no."

She walked with him as far as the old drive gate on the edge of the wood and watched him go. His mother, she sensed, was a memory which would never fade in him, and that had to be the same with his father. Some memories never died. You could learn to live with them, and to outlive the real anguish, but there could never be a day that did not bring some moment, some word, some note of music, some trivial turn of incident, some sight which did not bring the past back. She never heard now the sound of an R.A.F. fighter plane screaming low down the valley without memory rising sharp and anguishing for a moment or two in her. Then with a sense of self-anger she turned away, back towards the house. The past was the past, and if you dwelt with it too long you were doing no more than serving a self-imposed life sentence of useless regrets and growing self-pity.

102

*   *   *   *

From outside the caravan Peter shouted, "I'm off now, Dad."

Frank Courtney went to the door and looked out.

He said, "You sure you don't want me to come?"

"No, it's all right. Judy Preston said yesterday she would give me a hand. She's got to go on and get some eggs from Lady Diana. Not for eating. But for setting under a broody hen they've got. All right?"

"O.K."

He stood for a while in the doorway watching Peter move away towards the field gate. There wasn't any doubt in his mind that his son was enjoying himself here—which surprised him, because if ever there was a town boy Peter was one. But there you are, you never knew. They were always surprising you. Himself, he liked to have plenty of time to adjust to new people and new places. There was no gypsy in him. Still, he had to admit that he was more settled here than he had imagined he would be. The country was not his scene. But there was something about being perched up here with nothing but fresh air and miles of country around that not only gave you time to think things out, but to do it without rush. And rush was the word because that was what he had done when he had walked into the house and found Chris and Joan together. Just bloody well rushed out without a thought in his head but to get away. But since then he had had time to think—not only about them, but about Rundell and the whole French business. He had just panicked and run from both situations. Well, that period was over. Living up here, if only for the handful of days it had been, had calmed him and made him think logically. He'd have to go back sometime soon and clear up the whole messy business with Joan. Not go back to her to stay. That could never happen. But it was only sensible to put things in order between them. But before he could do that he knew that he would have to settle the Rundell affair. And that wasn't so easy. But the sooner it was done the better.

103

He went back into the caravan and read through the partly written letter he had been working on when Peter had called. Luckily in one of the caravan drawers he had found an old writing pad and he had his own biro with him. He hadn't found the writing easy. He didn't want to put the man's back up. On the other hand he didn't see why he had to do any crawling. He and the boy had been used ... well, perhaps not him so much. But certainly Peter. And, all right, he took part of the blame for that. He'd just been sheer bloody greedy and had closed part of his mind to the vague, but real enough truth.

He read: ... *and when I got back to England it was to find my wife in bed with another man. That's what finally set me off. But there was the other thing with the Count before that. The two together were too much for me. I couldn't know what was behind the French affair—but I can guess that something important the Count said, and probably dangerous, is locked up in Peter's memory. Now I want the whole thing cleared up so that the boy and I can start living again properly. I know the Count is dead, of course. Murdered. It was in the papers. Do you think I would have ever let the boy go near him if I'd ever had an inkling that it was all so high-powered secret as that? So the whole thing has got to be cleared up so that Peter and I can go on living peacefully. I've used some of the two thousand you gave me, but I'll square that up, and I'm not interested in the rest of the payment promised. But it has all got to be done safely so far as Peter is concerned. The Count, I guess, was murdered for what he had to say. Well, Peter knows it now and I want it out of his mind for good. And you're the only one I'm interested in talking to. Christ—how could I ever have closed my mind to the fact that it was all some dirty business? Anyway, what I want to do is this. I'll give you time to get this and then one evening I'll ring your flat and we can talk. But only with you. No one else there. I'll say I want to speak to Mr Archibald. If there's anyone with you you just say I must have the wrong number. This has got to be kept between us. No one else. And I'll be honest and say I know you may not be trustworthy either—but I've got to take that chance because I want Peter and myself to be able to walk free again and forget all this damned business.*

He picked up his biro and wrote—*And you'll have to come to wherever I say to get what you want. The boy and I are not going back to London until everything is tidied up. I hope all this is clear, and I'm quite genuine about it all.*

He signed it and sealed it in an envelope and then took out his wallet, found a card which Rundell had given him once, and addressed the letter.

As he put the envelope into his pocket—he didn't want Peter to get sight of it—he felt a slow sense of relief begin to stir in him. God, what a fool he had been in the first place . . . always wanting to show the boy off, so proud of him—and then letting himself, knowing damned well there was something fishy about it, be tempted just for the money. And perhaps not just for that. He knew himself and, lately, had come to acknowledge weaknesses to which for long he had turned a blind eye. The chief one being vanity. In himself he was nothing, just a small business man with no great gifts to bring him success. A moderately successful shopkeeper and no more. Not even any real love in him for the wares he sold. Just books—but how often did he ever read one? The daily and evening papers served him better. But when he had married pride had walked into his life, Sarah the radiant symbol of it, and with it—never entirely to be cleared from his mind—the wonder that she should ever have considered him worthy of her love. One miracle. And through her the gift of another. Peter. And there was no doubt in his mind that his strange gift of memory came from her. He had loved them both and, then, on losing Sarah, he had transferred all his affections to the boy—and out of vanity used him. Worse than that. Greed lay under the vanity. What had started as an occasional party game among friends he had slowly turned to a different account—not the making of the money so much as the opportunity as a father to draw to himself some of the credit for the boy's gift. Oh, Christ, yes—and the money. The bookshop had never done all that well. A living, a little more than barely, so that the odd twenty or fifty pounds from clubs or literary societies had been welcome. If by some miracle Sarah could walk in here now she would, without a word, spit in his eye and walk out, leaving him without need for any words to mark her contempt for him.

Putting the letter in his pocket, he walked out of the caravan into the late afternoon sunshine. Distantly down by the river a cuckoo called. Restless he walked along the edge of the trees until a turn in the old driveway brought into view Hightop Farm. It was a plain, ugly looking house, built of granite blocks and stood on its eminence like, he thought, some small fortress or perhaps prison ... though a small one. No place one would have expected a woman would choose to live in alone. Funny woman. She had been all bounce when she had first met them, a bit bossy. Perhaps putting on a bit of an act. It was no good always taking people on first looks, though. Everyone had their own way of starting off with strangers. It took a little while before you let your true self begin to come through. He knew that because he was like it himself. How are the mighty fallen. Once her family had owned everything the eye could see from here and then the good fortune and the good days had gone. Had all that made her turn her back on the world? That had been his first thought. But he was beginning to doubt it. She was still young. He could give her, he guessed, a good five years. And good-looking, though she dressed as though she just picked up the first thing that came to hand. Perhaps somewhere in the past—nothing to do with coming down in the world—something had happened. He suddenly grinned to himself. That was the story of so many people in the world. Somewhere in the past something had happened and left a load of grief, or self-disgust, or just a lack of spirit to care any longer.

Somewhere close at hand a small bird suddenly filled the air with a sharp, sweet song. Spring song, courting, nest-building, mating, the ineluctable cycle of life which Nature imposed. And not a one of them ever bothered with conscience or guilt or ugly thoughts that made sleep hard to find at night. To man alone had God given that burden and from the manner of his shouldering it the chance to prove himself and find Heaven. He smiled to himself at his mood and, as clearly as though she stood now at his side, could swear that he heard Sarah saying, as she so often had, "There's no sure way now of knowing how to get yourself a harp and the chance of learnin' to play it with the heavenly hosts. You have to find it for yourself through the brains and the conscience He started you off with."

Sarah ... she had to be up there among the saints. But if she weren't he knew she wouldn't be put down because she had known that God was willing to give you as many chances to try again as you wished. If you were a trier you were never turned away. He had to hang on to that. Whatever had gone wrong from his faults he had to find a way to put right.

*　　　*　　　*　　　*

Each carrying a large canvas shopping-bag, Peter and Judy Preston turned off the Sleadon road into the old driveway and began to climb the long hill slope through the woods. Peter, who had met Judy a few times now, liked her. She was about a year older than he was, a tallish, slim but strongly built girl, her black hair tied back in a pony's tail. She wasn't, he had thought the first time he had met her, a good-looker. But she had a nice face and warm brown eyes. She had some funny tricks too. When you asked her a question she had a way of closing her lips, blowing her cheeks out and then, with a little explosion through her lips, saying, "Well, 'tis like this..." And then whatever it was came. She didn't speak as broadly as her mother or father, but the West Country touch was there. And, more amusing too, she had a way of using the word "bugger" as though it were no swear word at all. He'd got used to it by now, but he knew that it put his father off sometimes. If a rabbit ran across their path she would say, "See that little bugger, Pete. He'd better keep out of my father's way." Or on finding a dead bird, "Poor little bugger. He's not properly feathered yet. Must have fallen out of his nest." He guessed too that when she realized that it made him laugh she put it on a bit because she was a great tease.

When they were some way up through the wood they sat down on a fallen tree to have a rest. She took a packet of cigarettes from her pocket, lit one, and then said, "I'm not going to give you one. But you can have a draw of mine if you like."

He grinned. "No thanks. Smoking is bad for your health. Says so on the packet."

"So's climbing up a hill with a big bag."

A little daring he asked, "What do your people think about you smoking?"

"Not much. Anyway I don't let 'em catch me. And, anyway, it's only just something I'm doing for a while like."

"Why?"

"Well, you got to try things, haven't you? To see if you like them?"

"And do you?"

"I'm not sure. Sometimes, yes. And sometimes, no. A lot of the other girls do. So I do—until I know whichways I really feel. You like living in London?"

"Yes, I do."

"What do you do there? When you're not at school?"

"Oh, not much. I used to have some rabbits. But they got stolen. People around us would steal anything. Then sometimes I go to the station. Paddington."

"What for?"

"Oh, to watch the trains and talk to people."

"Honest?"

"Yes."

"Sounds daft. My father went up once. Some years ago. He was in the Army, you know. And they had this big reunion thing in the . . . oh, something Hall."

"Albert Hall—"

"Aye, that's the bugger. But while he was away—and for sure someone must have heard him going on about his trip up in the pub and passed the word—the poachers came in and cleared three pools. All lovely clean-run fish. Just up they were. You should have heard him when he got back!"

"I've never seen a salmon. Not in the water, that is."

"You haven't? I don't believe it."

"It's true."

Judy stood up and threw her cigarette into the little stream that ran down the side of the driveway. "Come on. We've got plenty of time. I'll show you. Never seen a salmon! You poor little toad."

They left their bags by the stream and Judy led the way off

into the woods on their left, folllowing a narrow track. After a while the track dipped downhill through a stand of old oak trees and then came out on to a small bluff, covered with gorse bushes and tufty patches of heather and ling, which over-looked the river. Judy turned and said, "You've got to crawl from here, otherwise you may scare the beautiful little buggers. You never know. Sometimes they don't mind you just standin' there and looking. Another time—they get one peep of you and they're all over the place and gone. My father says there's only one thing certain about salmon and that is that you can never tell what they'll do. Come on."

She pulled him down and they began to crawl through the heather until they got to the lip of a high rock face that over-looked the pool. Judy said, "There now. Look down there towards the end of the pool where the water's all quiet and clear."

Peter looked down. The top end of the pool was foamy and disturbed where the river came over a small narrow fall into the pool. Lower down the pool the flow eased and the water was clear so that he could look right to the bottom.

"See 'em?"

"No, I can't," said Peter.

"You must be blind. They're a good dozen of the beauties."

She picked up a small stone and, as Peter watched, she flicked it into the lower end of the pool. At once Peter saw movement and then, as his eyes became used to looking into the water, he saw them. They were hanging there almost motionless in the eased current of the pool, grey-greeny shapes. Now and again one would turn away from its lie and move lower down the pool and there would be the sharp silver gleam of flanks and the sweep of a broad tail. They lay, he thought, for the most part so incredibly still that they were of the water itself, deceiving the eyes until they made the smallest movement ... the slow gaping of jaws to give a glimpse of white mouth or the strong, sudden sweep of a great tail.

He said almost to himself, "They're lovely ..."

"Aye," said Judy. "But there be some buggers that don't care for that. Price of salmon today and that lot down there are worth getting on for three hundred pounds. And there are more in the other pools like 'em. Two or three good poachers with their nets could clear this pool in half an hour. My father ever talk about poachers to you, don't you ever make any joke about it. Its no laughing thing for him. Now—" her tone changed and she reached for a large stone, "—disappearing trick." She tossed the stone into the pool and when the water settled there was no sign of a fish.

"They've all gone! Where?"

She stood up laughing. "They're still there. But you won't see them back for a while. They've all got their hiding places."

Later, when they got up to the caravan and Judy had gone on to Hightop Farm, Peter's father said that as they had come away in a hurry and were short of things—socks and shirts and so on—he thought it would be a good idea if they went to Plymouth on the bus the next day and did some shopping. Peter, who liked travelling even if it were only on a bus, was all for it and—on an impulse—asked if Judy could come with them.

"But she's got to go to school."

"Oh, Dad—don't be silly. It's Saturday tomorrow."

"Good Lord, is it?"

So, as Judy came back on her way home later, she was asked, and it was all fixed up. They walked down the next morning and picked her up and then climbed the short hill to the main road to catch the local bus to Tavistock and from there a coach to Plymouth.

It was one of the best days that Peter had had for a long time. To begin with it was nice to have someone else to talk to other than his Dad most of the time. And Judy looked smashing. She wore a tam o'shanter kind of thing on her head and was spruced up no end in a pleated skirt and a short red jacket over a white blouse and she wore highish-heeled shoes that made her walk a bit tottery. And they had fun—not just having lunch at a hotel on the Hoe in the window where you could look right out to sea—but afterwards when his Dad went off on his own to shop. They went across the Hoe to the Aquarium and made faces at the fish in the great glass-fronted tanks, and then down to the Barbican where the Pilgrim

Fathers had set sail for America to—as Judy said—give the poor buggers of Indians the rough edge of their tongue and take their land from them. She never minded what she said, and he knew his father liked her because he always laughed. And that was nice, too, because he hadn't gone in for a lot of laughing since they had left London.

With the money his father had given him he bought a little souvenir model of the Eddystone Lighthouse—which Judy had sworn she could see looking out from the hotel when they had lunch. He wasn't sure why or for whom he had bought the lighthouse. Perhaps for Joannie, he thought, if things got smoothed out ... though he didn't know about that. Anyway, he liked it, and if no one turned up ... well, he could keep it for himself and then always remember the day. A little sleepy in the coach going back—with Mr Preston coming to Tavistock—"And I want no argy about it, Mr Grady"—to pick them up, he lay back, hardly listening to his father chatting away to Judy. He tried to remember a day so good before. Ah, well, yes—with his mother. She used to keep him in fits until he ached. But with no one else since. Joannie was nice but she was awfully dumb about seeing a joke. And although he'd thought about it before this day, he couldn't really see them going back to Joannie. Something told him that his father would never do it ... Never ... He didn't understand all this business of being in love and getting married. Oh, yes—all the biology thing was simple and having babies. But how could you ever tell you were going to like someone enough to live with them all your life? Take Judy. He liked her a lot. But he was absolutely sure he wouldn't want to live with her all his life. There'd be fireworks in no time.

Mr Preston, Judy still with them, drove them right up to the caravan and stayed to have a drink with his father before leaving. When father and daughter left Peter was into bed and asleep well before they could have got back to their house.

His father sat on the doorstep of the caravan and slowly finished his drink. It had been a good day. Almost like some of the old days with Sarah. Well, you couldn't turn the clock back. Anyway, early next week Rundell would get his letter, posted in Plymouth, and then he could start to sort things out and find some way of beginning all over again.

*　　*　　*　　*

The letter was waiting for Mr Rundell when he came back late from his office on the Tuesday evening. He read it and then got up and made himself a drink and sat down and read it again. Then he put it in the large glass ashtray at his side and set fire to it.

He let the train of thought which the letter had re-started in his mind begin to run its course. The Comte de Servais—from the very nature of things, his past record, and from the intuitions of the people he had met and worked with—could, of course, have come to his end for any of a dozen reasons. And one of the reasons—which he had considered often—could be that in his own establishment there was someone whose loyalty was far, far less than any surface show appeared to indicate. Treason and deceit lay, since the time of Adam, in the hearts of all men and women. In the final analysis no one could be trusted. Including himself. No one—because if Adam had fallen when he already knew Paradise, what could mere men do whose only dream was to work for some lesser Paradise of their own? It could be Miss Lloyd. Or Teddy Tampion. Or a cipher clerk. Or the Minister himself. There was no way of looking at an apple and telling whether it held a breeding maggot. You had to bite it and see. On the other hand the Count could have died for the commonest of human reasons. Becoming the lover of another man's wife? (Thank God, he himself was a bachelor and had long dispensed with Eros.) Or, out of revenge, because he had once put a man and a family out of his farm. Idle to speculate. He had been murdered, he must assume, long had, because someone had known what he was about to do. They had missed the boat. Would have ways of knowing it. And—if they inhabited his world, and worked for him—would still be waiting for a chance to make sure that what only the boy knew stayed locked within him forever by death. One thing only was clear. He had a responsibility for the safety of the boy. Not so strong that—if circumstances forced him—he would never abandon it. But strong enough, backed by the pride he took in his own position and integrity, to rouse a ruthlessness and guile which were all of extreme passion he knew.

Well, then something must be done. He had few late evening appointments, the ballet and a club dinner. He would cancel them, and then each evening sit here late and wait. From now on he would handle Frank and Peter Courtney on his own.

*   *   *   *

Three nights later Frank Courtney telephoned Rundell. He had walked down to the Preston's cottage with Peter, who had been invited to have supper with Judy and some of her friends and listen to records afterwards. Leaving his son he went up the lane to the main Tavistock–Launceston road where he had noticed a call box close to a garage. He rang Rundell's number. It was some time before it was answered and then Rundell's voice came over, rather breathlessly.

Courtney said, "This is Mr Archibald here. Mr Rundell?"

"Yes—sorry to keep you waiting, but I was just about to get into a bath. I thought you'd phone much later."

"Are you alone?"

"Yes."

"Well, listen—first of all I want you to call off the police search for us. I won't go into how I know about it. If you want anything from us—then the search for us must be dropped."

"The moment I've finished speaking to you I'll arrange that—provided that you are going to co-operate sensibly."

"That's what I want to do. But I want your assurance that once that's done we'll be left alone for good."

"You have my promise—provided we get what we want."

"You can have it. But I've got to arrange it with Peter first. I don't want him to think that there's anything odd going on."

"Naturally. What do you suggest?"

"Well, I'll have to work it out now that I know you will ... well, forget all about us once you've got what you want."

"I'll be happy to do that. And I'll pay you what I promised."

"Well, we'll see about that. I guess you must know from the postmark on my letter that we're in the West Country somewhere?"

"I do."

"Then I suggest that you come down and stay at an hotel in Plymouth and when you're there I will arrange a meeting. I'll ring you again in a few days' time and you can tell me the name of the hotel and when you will be there."

"I'll do that. What will you tell your boy?"

"I don't know yet—but I'll work that out. There's just one thing. He doesn't know that the Comte de Servais is dead—and I don't want him to know."

"Naturally."

"I presume, too, that you know the first lines of the piece that the Count gave him?"

"Of course. And before you ring off I want to apologize for all the trouble you've had. I had no reason to believe that things would have gone so wrong."

"Nor had I—or I wouldn't be talking to you now. I'll ring you in a couple of days."

"Good. Oh—and there's something I want to tell you, about your wife and her so-called brother. Just a few enquiries we made."

Courtney listened as Rundell went on, and there was no surprise in him. When Rundell finished, he said, "Thank you. That clears up one of the messes, doesn't it? Goodbye."

Courtney put down the receiver and stepped out of the box. The May night was darkening, and the cloudless sky was brightly stippled with stars. Suddenly a shooting star blazed briefly across the heaven and with it came poignantly a memory of Sarah. So had a star fallen the night on Hampstead Heath, searing across the London sky, when she had told him she was pregnant and he had said it had to be a happy omen for the coming child. He could hear her voice now ... *'Tis no such thing. One of the heavenly harp players up there has just nipped out between numbers, taken a quick draw on his fag and tossed it away as he went back*. He could hear her laugh now at his shocked face. Well, maybe she was right in a way. He had never ceased to be surprised by her naturalness. She carried heaven with her and saw it in her own terms.

He walked back to the caravan, passing the Preston's cottage and hearing the sound of music, and toiled up the long woodland drive, the sound of the running stream filling the night with gentle water music. Relief was in him. And when all this business was over ... soon over ... he and Peter would start on a new life.

CHAPTER EIGHT

IT WAS TEN o'clock before Peter left the Preston's cottage. Mr Preston and Judy had offered to walk part of the way up to the caravan with him, but he had said no. Not because he hadn't wanted them to, but because to have accepted would have shown that walking up through the woods late at night did come somewhat scary—even if you knew perfectly well that the sounds came from birds and beasts going about their natural ways.

He had enjoyed the evening, and the dancing to a tape recorder—though he wasn't much good at it. But he had begun to get the hang of it after a while. Judy had helped, showing him what to do. But he could see that she was soft on another boy there. A nice chap with red hair and a mouth organ, on which, for a change from the recorder, he played old tunes and they all sang. And then Mr Preston came in and gave them riddles.

> Four stiff standers,
> Four down-hangers,
> Two lookers, two crookers,
> One dirty switch about lags behind.

Which was a cow, of course. And then—

> The man that made it didn't want it
> The man that bought it didn't need it
> The man that used it didn't know it.

Which was a coffin. And then Mrs Preston came and took

him away before he began to get saucy. He had never been to a party like it before. All the young people there knew one another, and their families had mostly lived round about for generations. It was all different from London. When the boys left school at the end of the day they scattered all over the place and you never saw them until the next morning. Round about here people stayed put and everybody knew everybody. Although he wasn't sure whether he really cared for that, because he liked to go off and be by himself, he had to admit that it made a change. Still, it would be nice to get back to London. If they went to live over the shop that would be all right. He would be glad, too, not to have to keep on remembering that his name was Grady. Once or twice he had almost come unstuck over that. If you were a real criminal on the run, he thought, it would be the easiest thing in the world to give yourself away.

Mooning away to himself he went slowly up the rough drive, glad of the company the rushing little stream made. But when he was some way up it his attention was caught by something shining in the starlight in a little clearing just off the drive where the stream curled away from it in a small bow. He walked over to it and saw to his surprise that it was a rather knocked about motor car with a few old sacks draped over it. His eyes had been caught by the metallic gleam from one of the headlights off which a sack had slipped. He stood there for a moment or two puzzled, and then put out his hand and felt the radiator. It was still warm.

He went down the side of the car and looked in the back. There was just enough light from the stars in the cloud-clear sky for him to see a pile of old sacks on the back seat and on the floor a long pole with the curved hook of a rusty old fishing gaff wired to it. For a moment or two he just stood looking into the car and then turned and ran back to the drive and into the bushes on the other side. He sat in their cover, wondering what he should do. He knew exactly what must be going on for the car was parked just opposite the point in the drive where Judy had turned off to show him the salmon in the big pool. He guessed that there must be poachers down there at this moment taking fish.

Almost without knowing he was doing it, he stood up and began to follow the narrow track down to the river. When he came to the edge of the tree line above the river, he went down on his stomach and wriggled through the heather and scrub at the top of the rocky bluff which overhung the pool. One look told him all he wanted to know. There were four men working the pool. Two were in wet suits in the water and two others, one just below him and the other on the far side of the river, working the net. As he watched he saw two great salmon jump, the water cascading from them like silver in the starlight.

Without waiting to see more he crawled back to the trees and then began to run. It took him a good twenty minutes to get back to the Preston's cottage, and—since everyone had now gone to bed—it was some time before Mr Preston came down to the door, hitching the braces of his trousers up and tucking in the ends of his shirt.

"Good Lord, lad—what brings you back here?"

"Mr Preston—there's poachers. They were in the big pool that Judy took me to and ... and ... they've got a car up there ..."

"Have they, by God! Then I'll get the car and be after them."

But at this moment, Mrs Preston, coming up behind him in her dressing gown, said, "That you won't, Bert Preston. There'll be four of 'em at least and you one man. Was they drawing the net, Peter?"

"I think so. The fish were jumping. And, anyway, Mr Preston could ring the police because they won't get far in that old car. I got its number—and I did something else. You know, to stop them getting far away. After all it was the only thing I could do because I guessed they wouldn't come down the drive again. They'd go out by the top meadow gate on to the side road up there—"

"Steady, steady, lad. Now let's hear. You got their number?"

"Yes."

"And the other thing?"

"Well, there was an old tin lying by the stream so I took it and filled it with gravel and water and tipped it down through the petrol tank filler. I did it three times. Then put the cap back and ... and—" He paused, panting for breath.

At this moment, and despite his own excitement Peter was delighted to hear it, Mrs Preston put an arm round him and drew him into the cottage, saying, "Well, if you ain't the clever little bugger now!" Then turning to her husband she said, "Now you get on to the police and tell them. They'll pick 'em up, wherever they are. And then you can drive up and tell his father I'm keeping him down here for the night."

He slept in the spare bed in Judy's room, and it was a long time before they finished talking and went to sleep. Just before he did, Judy said sleepily, "What made you think of that water and gravel dodge?"

"Oh, that..." He was calm now and rather pleased with himself. "Well, where I live in London, round Praed Street way, the coloured boys do that sometimes if they don't like someone."

The next morning brought its rewards and excitements too. Mr Preston came in and said that two police patrol cars had picked up the poachers just as they were about to abandon their broken down car. "Not that that'll put the fish back in the river though."

Later—as Peter was about to leave for the caravan—a photographer-reporter arrived from the local newspaper to interview him and take a photograph. He took a photograph, too, of Peter with Mr Preston and he was amused that Mrs Preston made her husband put a tie on and his best jacket before he was taken.

Then Mr Preston drove him up to the caravan. On the way he said, "It'll all be in the local paper tomorrow. You'll be a hero."

"I'm not that. I really was scared they'd see me and get after me."

"That's not the point. Every mortal being gets scared at times like that. The hero bit is that, no matter for all that, you kept your head and thought about that water and gravel trick."

His father—though he had known not to worry when he had not come back to the caravan—was pleased that he had kept his head. But when Bert Preston told him about the newspaper reporter and the photographs he had taken, Peter thought he looked a bit old-fashioned. After Mr Preston had left Peter asked, "Didn't you want them to photograph me? After all, it's only the local paper and Joan won't ever see that to find where we are. And I did remember to say my name was Grady."

"No, that's all right, son. It's just that ... well, those men might have got hold of you and done you some harm." Then he grinned and went on, "No, I'm very proud of you." He put his arm around him and gave him a hug.

When he went up to Hightop Farm later for their daily milk, Lady Diana gave him a big welcome, for she already had heard the news from Bert Preston, and said, "See the conquering hero comes! Well done, young Peter. And it all calls for a celebration. Tell your father I'd be honoured if the two of you would come and have dinner with me tomorrow evening. But you needn't walk all the way back here this morning to tell me. I'll give you time to get back to the caravan and ask him. Then I'll walk to the wood gate and fire my gun and you can dip the caravan flag twice to say Yes."

Grinning, Peter asked, "And what if we aren't going to come, ma'am?"

She laughed. "Then you can just pull the flag right down and pack your bags and go. Also it'll be a disappointment for Judy Preston. I was going to ask her to come and join us and stay the night up here."

Peter laughed. "Don't worry about the flag, your Ladyship." Then after a moment of thought, his voice changing, he said, "How can men do things like that? Just netting and killing all those fish. They're so beautiful to look at."

She shook her head. "God knows, Peter. Some do it for gain—and plenty of others for sport. One's wrong and the other is considered right. But if you were to ask the salmon about it you could guess what their answer would be. They die just the same."

When he got back to the caravan Peter told his father about the invitation and half expected him to grumble a bit about it before saying *Yes*. But to his surprise his father smiled and said, "Why not? A little company would do us both good."

At that moment there came the sound of a gun being fired at the far end of the woods and Peter ran out to dip the caravan flag.

In those few moments, while the boy was gone from him, and for no reason or sudden emotion on which he could lay his hands—though maybe prompted, he felt, by the reasonable chance that soon everything would be cleared up with Rundell—Frank Courtney less came to a conclusion than found it already with him, hardened and not to be ignored. In more ways than he could comfortably consider he knew that he had not been a very satisfactory father since the death of Sarah and his marriage to Joan. The heart had gone from him and he had in many ways almost changed personality—and not for the good. But now, in a little while, the tablets would be wiped clean and he could make a fresh start with the boy. It was no good fudging issues any longer and trying to keep things from Peter. Young people might not have old heads on their shoulders, but many of them had an instinctive wisdom beyond their years, and a capacity for understanding that most adults—certainly himself—under-rated.

With Rundell out of the way he wanted a clean slate for himself and Peter, so that they could live in sanity and decency, himself harbouring no deceits to eat like woodworms into the solid foundations of their relationship. The only sane answer to any problem was to state its truth clearly and take the consequences. His boy was growing up fast and already had a certain wisdom which he himself had never had at that age. He deserved almost at any cost ... no, at any cost ... to have the truth. To have the truth and to deal with it according to his own fashion ... emotionally and rationally. He was ready for it. Last night must have filled him with panic, but not to the extent that he had lost his head and just taken to his heels. In his fright he had still been able to think. He had to know the truth about Joan and Chris; to know it and then clear

it from his mind. Keeping it from him was over-protecting him
and forcing him to weave a web of lies for the boy's comfor
when, in fact, the real comfort lay in the truth. And the
moment to do it was the earliest moment. Fifteen minutes ago
the thought of doing it would have distressed him and given
rise to excuses for not facing and sharing the facts with the boy
Suddenly there was a lift of spirits in him which he had no
known for months . . . years.

Peter came back in and sat down across the narrow table
from him and said, "I don't really know what it means, do
you, Dad? That know yourself. *Nosce teipsum.* How can you no
know yourself?"

Courtney was silent for a moment and then put out a hand
and rubbed his knuckles down the side of Peter's sun-browned
face. As he did so Sarah's voice came clearly to him in
memory . . . *God waits up there and sighs the long sigh of eternity
dear Holy Father, at all the people turning to him to help them out of
their troubles when they only have to look within themselves to find th
answer tucked away inside themselves like a nugget of gold.*

He said, "Well, it doesn't mean that you don't know who
you are and things about yourself like where you live and what
kind of foods you like or don't like."

"Then what does it mean?"

"I think it means to know exactly what kind of person you
are . . ." He hesitated, searching for an example and then wen
on, "For example, when you saw that old car of the poachers
parked on the drive, and knew what it was most likely al
about—well, you could have said it was none of your busines
and just come up here and kept quiet."

"But they were after Mr Preston's salmon! I couldn't jus
take no notice of that. He worships his fish and looks afte
them."

"I know he does. And what you've just said is part o
knowing yourself. You found out that you had the kind of se
that doesn't like to stand by and see hurt or harm done t
others by bad people."

Peter laughed. "But of course I don't. Still, I don't see wh
you have to put that on a flag and tell all the world about it."

122

"Let's forget the flag, shall we? Suppose for instance you got into trouble. Say you got tempted one day and stole something from ... well, May's kiosk at Paddington, and you fancied she hadn't seen you, but she had and as you were going she said, 'Come off it, Peter. What do you think you're up to?' What would you do?"

Peter laughed. "Oh, Dad, I wouldn't be so daft. Fancy trying a thing like that on May! She's got eyes in the back of her head."

"You mean you would steal, if you wanted something badly and thought you could get away with it?"

"No, not any more."

"What do you mean—not any more?"

"Well, I did it once in the newsagents in Praed Street. You know, Mrs Harper. There was this aeroplane model kit and she went out the back to answer the phone—so I put it in my school bag. But I felt awful about it and I'd only gone a little way up the street when I had to go back and tell her."

"And what did she say?"

"Not much. I mean about the stealing. She just said to keep it and pay her so much a week out of my pocket money. Only I didn't pay her. She's got a collecting box in there for the blind or something. She used to make me put it in there and when I'd paid it all back she said sort of ... well, that if I ever felt like stealing anything again to remember that there were a lot of people in the world who wanted things worse than I did who'd never be able to do anything about it. But, Dad, why are you talking to me about all this?"

"Well, in a way you started it all by asking about *Know Thyself*. Because, very often, I've tried not to know myself because I wanted to do things or have things which I fancied."

"Like what?"

"Well, this memory thing of yours. Although I don't understand it I'm very proud of you for it. But then I saw how I could make a little money by it ... you know, by taking you round to all those places to show you off to people."

"But I liked that. And I knew you could do with the money because the shop doesn't do all that good. Really, Dad, if that's all, it's nothing."

"Yes, but say I'd got you into danger by doing it?"

"How could you? It's only a trick sort of thing in my mind. What danger could there be?"

For a few fleeting seconds Courtney considered going on and telling the truth and then he knew that he could not. He had no right to try and shift part of his burden on to the boy. To cover his uneasiness, he laughed and said, "Well, none. But what I wanted to tell you was that Mr Rundell paid me a lot of money for us to go to France and see the Comte de Servais and let him give you a memory test in French. And I feel ... well, I can't keep his money unless you see him some time and we finish the job."

"No, of course you can't. But we can do that when we get back to London, can't we?"

"Well, before then. You see I had to telephone him and explain about our coming away ... because of Joannie. And he said that he was coming to Plymouth soon and would you do it for him there?"

Peter laughed. "Well, of course. I like going to Plymouth. Can Judy come with us again, too?"

"I should think so." Courtney was silent for a while. The whole talk had gone quite differently from the way he had imagined it would. The chief thing he had wanted to clear up was the Joan business. At any time he could have relied on Peter going to Plymouth with him to see Rundell. A sudden spurt of anger with himself made him speak out, almost harshly, "And there's something else I want to say to you. I was never properly married to Joan. She's not really your stepmother."

To his surprise Peter laughed and said, "Oh, Dad—you're pulling my leg. I went to the wedding in that funny old office place. You mean that wasn't a proper marriage like having it in a church?"

"No, I don't mean that. I mean that Joannie was already married to Chris—only she thought he was dead, lost overboard a year before we met. But he wasn't and when he came back she pretended he was her brother."

"Really?"

124

"Yes, really."

Peter laughed. "Coo—wait until I tell May about this. She'll have a good laugh. You should hear her go on about sailors and seamen. She says they only go to sea to sober up and then come back for more. Her brother was in the Navy, you know. He was torpedoed twice and she says he's still drinking heavily to try and get the taste of salt out of his mouth and—" Peter paused and then in a serious tone went on, "But Dad that means you can get married again. And we don't have to hang about down here because it doesn't matter that Joannie is looking for us because she's got her proper husband back."

At this point Frank Courtney gave up. He had done his best, perhaps without a very clear idea of what it was he had wanted to say and the whole thing had run off Peter like water from a duck's back.

He said, rather wearily, "Well, we mustn't rush things. We've got to see Mr Rundell in Plymouth first. I arranged all that over the telephone some time ago."

"Oh, that's all right. I don't mean rush back right away. I'm enjoying it down here—but not for ever. I wouldn't want that." Peter paused, and then said gravely, "Isn't that funny? I asked you about Know Thyself and all this came out and I don't know any more about myself, but I know a lot more about other people." He sighed and then said, "Well, bugger me..."

Courtney laughed, reached forward and pulled his ear, and said, "You use that word anywhere outside of Sleadon and I'll flay you."

* * * *

Eating his breakfast in the hotel dining room Albert Horsfell was mildly irritated at the constant music being fed into the room by the hotel musak system. He had no ear for music and liked to eat in reasonable quietude. Food, good or bad, should be enjoyed with the minimum of outside interference. His cereals had been limp instead of crisp, the toast soggy, the bacon overcooked and the eggs underdone. He felt that all this could be the preamble to a day of further trials and disappointments. Not that he took disappointments or bad food hard. Experience had taught him how to cushion them with hope. Where there was hope there was life. Or death. It was irritating, too, that the London papers were late and he had been deprived of his *Daily Mail*—which meant missing the Snoopy cartoon. Today he would finish off the second of the segments he had marked out on his map. It would be work for which he now had a flagging enthusiasm. There were times on this kind of assignment when conviction began to harden that the glittering prize would be withheld ... no gentle lick of a thumb ball to wet the foresight, no beautifully drawn out pause while hands and eyes steadied, no moments of exquisite satisfaction as the shot echoes rolled like young thunder. He made a private bet with himself that another day and they would call him off. They always got so impatient. Mean over wasting their money.

The waitress with a dirty apron and a run in the left leg of her tights asked him if he would like more coffee and he said he would. As she poured for him he asked if the London papers had arrived and she shook her head and said, "Sorry, sir. Boy hasn't come with them yet."

The boy, he thought, ought to be bastinadoed when he did condescend to come. When he'd been a boy if he put a foot wrong, and often when he had not, he had taken it on the arse from his father. Mixing discipline with pleasure. He sighed. The good old days—they left their mark, transient on the flesh but permanently on the spirit.

The waitress came back and put a crumpled newspaper in front of him and said, "You might like yesterday evening's local, sir."

"Ah, that's very kind of you."

He shook and smoothed the paper into some neatness and glanced at the front page. Let us see, he thought, how the world of Tavistock and environs has been wagging. Who fined for driving without lights, tax disc or too much alcohol; what frustrated yokel has raped which unwary maiden and which councillor has fulminated against the iniquity of suggesting that new council houses should be built anywhere but on the plot of land which his brother owned, purely, of course, as a nominee for himself. A ten-minute dip into local life before he took to the highways and byways in search of game while his ears were gladdened by the sound of bird song and the liquid music of running and babbling brooks.

His thoughts were broken as his eyes caught a photograph of a young boy standing at a garden gate, a glimpse of a cottage behind him, and over it a headline—*Holiday Boy Foils Salmon Poachers*. And then, underneath the photograph, the beginning of the account. *Young Peter Grady holidaying with his father in a caravan near Sleadon by his resource and quick thinking brought about the downfall of a gang of poachers ...*

He read the account through, and then sat back and shook his head in mild but happy wonder. Sometimes the dark gods were good. One small incident led to another. Or perhaps more accurately, one small boy led to another. The hotel paper boy, dawdling and late with the London papers, and here— due to the kindness of the waitress—had popped up another small boy, and undoubtedly the one he wanted. All was not chaos in the Universe; sometimes there seemed overwhelming evidence of design either for good or bad. Personally he had a feeling that the gods didn't care much which, just so long as they could keep the human pot bubbling away for their unfathomable amusement.

An hour later he turned off the main road and drove down to Sleadon, past the Preston's cottage and then up the hill until he was free of the woods on his left. Not far along the road he came to a gateway to a meadow, rich with thistles and clumps of flowering rushes. High above the air was full of lark song. There was a style at the side of the gate and a ramblers' sign-post which read—*Hightop Woods and River Walk. Please keep to path.* He slung his field-glasses round his neck, locked the car and climbed the style. Time spent on reconnaissance ... an echo of his National Service army days floated into his mind ... is seldom wasted. And a lovely morning for it, too. The snail was on the thorn and God in His Heaven. As he walked a hare started up from the shelter of a patch of rushes and went zigzagging away from him. The hare was wise and knew the rules of the survival game. Never let yourself be a sitting target and when you run never run straight. But the boy wouldn't be like that. Innocence under the strengthening summer sun.

He wouldn't do it today, of course. Oh dear no. When it happened everything would have to go like clockwork and his line of retreat—not escape for no one would follow—securely marked out in his mind. Bill paid at the hotel that morning yet to come, tips given, and hope you've enjoyed your stay, sir. Indeed, indeed.

He went through the gate at the far side of the meadow and on to an old driveway. He passed the caravan with little more than a glance, but it was enough. A man was standing in the doorway, smoking, and a boy—the boy—was coming back from the stream carrying a bucket full of water. He gave them both a wave and the boy waved back and the man just nodded at him. High above a flag flapped half-hearted in the lazy breeze. He went on down the driveway, saw the roof of some building showing above the far trees and to avoid it turned down a small track to his left towards the river. When he reached the river he struck the fishing path and turned up the river. Somewhere along here, he presumed, the heroic poaching incident had taken place. The path rose to a steep bluff over a wide pool and he sat down and polished the lens of his field-glasses. For half an hour he sat and enjoyed himself. It was a good place for bird-watching. A dipper, a kingfisher, a mallard duck—nesting somewhere around for sure—and a heron that came planing down between the trees and took up its archaic fishing stance in the shallows at the bottom of the pool.

Half an hour later, as he was thinking of moving on to check the high ground above the caravan, the gods sent him a bonus. It had happened before in his career, more times, he felt, than could be accounted for by accident. Somewhere some dark god over the years had taken a kindly interest in his work. There was the sound of movement to his left and the boy came down a small track through the trees and out on to the bluff over the water. Seeing him the boy, with the natural ease and friendliness of the young, came to him and said, "I saw you just now, didn't I? You went by the caravan."

"That's right." A nice boy, natural, no stupid shyness or awkwardness. "You on holiday in the caravan?"

"Yes. With my father."

Poor father, he thought—soon to be bereaved. But then, grief passes and only the good memories linger on. He asked, "Do you come down here often?"

"Yes. Now and again. I like it here. What do you do with those glasses? Watch birds?"

"That's it. Our little feathered friends. There was a heron down there just now—but he took off when he heard you coming."

"I'm sorry, sir."

"No need to be. I don't rate herons very high in the scale of rarities. Now, if you'd frightened off a red-crested, three-legged popinjay, I would have been annoyed."

The boy laughed. "I'll bet. Well, I won't stay and frighten off any more. I'm really on my way down to pick up our groceries."

"How often do you do that?"

"It depends. Two or three times a week. Bye."

When he was gone Albert Horsfell sat thinking for a while. Then he moved back up the path the boy had come down and finally found the place he wanted. From the shelter of a large rank growth of rhododendron bushes to screen him he could cover the top of the overhanging river bluff where he had talked with the boy. Fifty or sixty yards. One shot enough. And now, thanks to the boy's co-operation, he had been saved a lot of work. There's a destiny that shapes our ends ... he thought. So be it. And nobody took much notice of the sound of a shot around here. Always some keeper after rabbits or vermin. Nice boy, but it was no good being sentimental. That had all departed from him years ago. Anyway, there hadn't been much to depart, because his father had knocked most of that out of him before he even got into long trousers.

Walking back to his car, he decided that he would give it two days' rest. They'd want more groceries by then for sure ... and anyway, it wasn't only the groceries that brought the boy down. Two days. He telephoned that evening from a call box to London.

"I've picked the boy up. It'll be done two or three days from now."

"Good. Let us know when it's done."

Conversations with his employers, he thought, as he left the box, were always brief. But the money was good. Yet money wasn't everything. There were times when he wondered what an assignment was all about. You were never told. Still there were compensations. Walking up through the woods he had picked up a merlin briefly in his field glasses. Lovely ... he hadn't seen one for over two years. Where had that been ...? Ah, yes. In a pine tree on the heath near Sandhurst. What had he been doing there? Bothered if he could remember ... Oh, yes, taking in his sights one of the cadet officers ... a dusky-coloured number from somewhere in darkest Africa, son of some jumped-up tyrant. Nice, friendly boy—not the cadet officer—this one. And for sure from his manner not one whose father took a delight in raising red welts across his poor little backside.

*   *   *   *

When Teddy Tampion telephoned that evening on his way to his club, he was told the news passed by Albert Horsfell. He came out of the box, whistling gently to himself and feeling happiness springing in him. On the list or not—it didn't matter now. Well, if anything ever did rate a bottle of *Pol Roger* with his dinner this did. And after that ...? Perhaps he would pay a little visit to Mayfair and the scented charms and pleasures of some fair lady.

CHAPTER NINE

As TAMPION WALKED happily towards his club, Rundell was in the Minister's room at Whitehall. The Minister was in full evening dress, with decorations, for he was shortly to leave for a dinner at the Mansion House where he knew he would enjoy the food and wine but have to conceal his yawns during the speeches afterwards. He smiled at Rundell and said, "Yes, of course, I approve of your going to Plymouth to see the boy. But I think we should take certain precautions, don't you? In fact, I rather fancy that's why you have come to see me. No?"

"Yes, it is, Minister. I'm far from happy about this affair. It would be less than common-sense to assume that our internal security is sound—not after the death of the Comte de Servais. There's been a leak somewhere. I don't say necessarily from our side, but from somewhere. It would be unfortunate if on my way to Plymouth, or there, something happened to me because I am the only one who knows the Count's opening lines."

"The key to our young friend's memory. What a world where you sometimes feel that if you should talk in your sleep your wife may hear and turn out to be no longer a loving spouse but ... well, shall we say, just another red in the bed? Dear, dear, I sometimes wish I'd gone into big business as my father wished. There at least the first flash of the knife gives you a little warning. So what do you suggest?"

Rundell smiled. "The only thing I can suggest. That I trust the one man in the world who has never given me the slightest doubt of his integrity and love of country."

"I say now, Rundell, don't give me that kind of rotund talk. I shall get enough of that tonight. I always need at least two glasses of Château Lafite before I can take it. I presume you mean me, of course."

"Who else?"

"Must it be? You know I have a shocking memory."

Rundell laughed. "But you have a very secure safe."

"Ah ... what stratagem portends?"

"I've taped it for you. Just a couple of lines." He pulled from his pocket a small tape cassette and put it on the table in front of him. Then, with a smile, he went on, "I think you'll find my accent quite good. A little point of personal pride that, of course."

The Minister came over and picked up the cassette and with a sigh said, "What a sad world we live in. So I lock this away until I hear that you've got what you want?"

"Until I have personally reported to you, face to face, what I've got. I apologize for the tautology of *personally* and *face to face*. Sometimes under strain syntax becomes a victim."

"And not under strain always, dear Rundell. You should read some of the department minutes I get. And worse, hear some of the Guildhall speeches I endure. God gave us speech to set us apart from the animals and to be able to glorify His works. And what happens? The world is returning to mumbles and grunts and His Churchmen are re-writing the glorious language of Cranmer in the absurd conviction that the average mental age of congregations is between eight and fourteen. However, I will gladly become the custodian of your little cassette. And when do you go to Plymouth?"

"I'm awaiting a call from the boy's father. As you know, Minister, he came back to a rather traumatic situation at home."

"Unless we are very lucky, it happens to us all at some time or another."

The Minister was silent for a while, his fingers fidgeting at the set of his dress tie. Then he said, "You're of course taking someone to Plymouth with you?"

"I hadn't thought to."

"My dear Rundell, that's not like you. The boy spills everything to you—and then Fate steps in ... knocked over by a bus, train accident. Then where are we? You must take someone. Either Tampion or Miss Lloyd, I leave the choice to you. If one or other of them is a traitor where would your money go?"

"God knows. Miss Lloyd perhaps—she went to France, arranged it all."

"Well, I leave the choice to you. And now I must kick you out. I have to be away to take turtle soup, a highly over-rated delicacy, and all the other Lucullan delights which we are bribed with to endure the ensuing tedium." He sighed and then went on, "I know you'll forgive my saying this but, my dear Rundell, next time remember the maxim of all actors— don't get mixed up in a show with small children or animals."

*　　*　　*　　*

Dinner at Hightop Farm was just finishing, and Peter was enjoying himself. He and his father had smartened themselves up as much as they could from their limited wardrobe. Lady Diana looked almost a different person. She wore a nice black dress, gold earrings and she had painted her nails red and wore her hair in a different way. It was really a bit hard to imagine her as he usually saw her ... slopping around wearing any old thing. Judy didn't look different all that much, but she'd got on a nice blue-and-white striped dress and wore a bracelet with a collection of silver charms on it. And so far he hadn't heard her use the word 'bugger' once and didn't expect her to because he guessed her mother would have given her a lecture about it before coming out.

The house, too, was not what he had expected. So far he had never been beyond the kitchen which was always in a mess. But once you passed that you were in a different world. Everything was polished and sparkling. Nice old furniture and pictures of hunting and country scenes, and a lot of paintings of Lady Diana's ancestors. You could tell that because there was a likeness to her in some of the women.

They had omelette to begin with which Judy cooked, and then roast beef, Yorkshire pudding, baked potatoes and peas.

Frozen, of course, but—as her Ladyship said—out of her own garden and put down in the freezer. Then peaches, and thick cream from her own cow. He drank water because he didn't like wine much. But the others all drank it and he could see towards the end of the meal it was making Judy a bit gay. Not that she needed anything much to do that.

Then, after all that, they left everything as it was in the dining room and had coffee in a small sitting room, which wasn't quite as tidy. Joannie would have fussed no end about the magazines and papers lying about. But he liked it, especially the old guns and fishing rods on the walls—and a stuffed salmon of enormous size in a case over the bookshelf which Lady Diana said one of her brothers had caught.

But the best thing was that he could see that his father was enjoying himself. He was much more like he used to be before . . . well, he was not going to think about that. But it did occur to him fleetingly that now Joannie didn't belong to them in any way it would be really something if his father married someone like Lady Diana, someone who really laughed when she laughed, and didn't care a button if you knocked a glass over or got a bit mixed up with what fork or spoon to use. But his father marrying a Lady was out of the question. His father couldn't become a Lord or a Sir or whatever it was, and certainly Lady Diana wouldn't want to be a plain Mrs. Still it was quite a nice idea to think about. Then, after they'd had coffee, Judy said that he and she would clear away the dining-room and do the washing up. He thought that was going it a bit much but he didn't show it.

They carried everything out of the dining room. Judy knew where it all went and was pretty bossy, as though it were her own place, telling him what to do and where to put things. And forgot herself once and called him a "silly bugger" for dropping one of the good glasses which, fortunately, landed on a cushion in the dog's basket by the sink.

As he picked it up, she said, "You know what?"

"Know what what?"

"About your father."

"What about him?"

"Well, I thought he was sort of stuffy. You know, the keep to yourself kind. But he's not. Least not when he's had a glass or two of wine. That was funny about the Australian in his bookshop, wasn't it? Her Ladyship nearly laughed her head off."

"So did I the first time I heard it," said Peter. It was one of his father's favourite but not very good jokes about a man a little drunk who had come into the shop and taken a book down from a shelf and started to read it upside down. When his father jokingly had said it must be difficult to read like that the man had said, 'No problem, Pommie. In Australia we always read this way.'

"Her Ladyship likes him. Which isn't usual. Fur and feather is all she cares for. I can't think why she asked you two up here."

"Oh, thanks."

"Well, what I mean is—she isn't one for company. Not since her fiancé died, years ago. He was in the R.A.F. and he crashed. My goodness, he was a goer. My father said he had the best hands for horse, rod or gun he'd ever known."

"She must have been very sad. My mother died you know. I missed her a lot. But you get over it, you know. Well, not right over it, but enough. What are we going to do when we've finished this lot?"

"I'll tell you. We'll let them go on talking in there and I'll borrow the cassette player and I'll teach you to dance."

"You jolly won't."

"I jolly will. You don't know what you're missing. What are you going to do when you fall in love with a girl and can't take her to a dance and look into her eyes and say, 'Oh, bugger me, me dear, if you ain't the most beautiful thing on two legs that ever walked'?"

He laughed, but he got his own back when she was showing him how to follow the music for he suddenly stopped, looked into her eyes and said, "Oh, bugger me, me dear, if you ain't the most beautiful thing on two legs that ever walked." And then they both collapsed on to the window seat, laughing their heads off.

Hearing the sound of music and of the two young people in

the kitchen laughing, Lady Diana said, "That's something this house hasn't heard for a long time. They get on well, don't they?"

Courtney laughed. "That's Peter all over. He always gets on well with people. Sometimes I think too well. He just takes people at their face value. Sees good in all things. Full of trust . . ."

"You make it sound as though that weren't a wise thing to do."

"No, not entirely. So long as you are prepared for the bump when someone lets you down."

She was silent for a moment or two. She liked him. He was an attractive man. Not that that meant much to her these days. But, at least, it was pleasant to have someone here who just accepted her and her circumstances and never once out of understandable human curiosity moved over the line of good taste to satisfy their curiosity about her. She could say it to herself now without any disturbance . . . still young and presentable enough to respond to the pull of her own instincts and appetites.

She laughed quietly and said, "That sounds rather gloomy."

"Oh, I didn't mean it to. And anyway it's a fact that most of our troubles we bring on ourselves. For a variety of reasons which in the beginning seem O.K.—or you make them seem like it. Why is it—No, I can't ask you that question."

"If you don't I shall understand. But I wish you would because if ever I've seen a man less enjoying what is supposed to be a holiday, it's you. Peter goes off and enjoys himself. Makes friends. But—and this is a matter of simple observation—you do nothing. You sit on the caravan step and smoke. You walk up and down the driveway. And I don't think for a moment you're seeing or hearing much that goes on around you. Am I right?"

"Possibly." He smiled. "But I don't mind."

She shrugged her shoulders. "Well, then. Why don't we have a cosy gossip about it? I always was a one for rushing fences. Give yourself time to think and you never jump. That happened to me. I had the world in front of me so that I almost thought that the larks went on singing all night. And then I lost the man I loved and the world turned upside down. I just withdrew. I know it was a mistake now, but it's become a habit—like a nice, warm overcoat against perpetual winter. You never realize it's summer again and you don't need it."

He looked at her in silence for a moment or two, and perhaps for the first time saw her as she was, as a face and a person to remember, as someone perhaps who was in need of open communion in the way he needed it. Communion was it, or perhaps on his side confession? Father, I have sinned and done those things which I ought not to have done...

Then he laughed, and said, "Why should I bore you to tears with my problems?"

"If they begin to, I'll tell you."

He got the impression at that moment, although he could give her a few years, and she was a damned fine-looking woman, that she was infinitely older in wisdom and understanding than he was. How many times had he known the same with Sarah? And, anyway, there was nothing in all he could say that would harm anyone—except himself. She wouldn't think much of him afterwards, but it would have been a relief to offer himself up to condemnation.

With a shrug of his shoulders, he said, "Well, I'll tell you a not very pretty story—that's if the children stay out there long enough."

"They will." She nodded to the table at his side with its decanter and his glass. "Help yourself to more brandy—not for courage. But it's helpful to have a glass to fiddle with and sip at."

"Thank you."

She watched him pour his brandy, heard the sound of laughter and music from the kitchen, and for a moment—before she thrust it sharply from her—thought of another man who once had often sat there, slim, and hard-bodied, dark-haired and with eyes that were always creased with laughter. That loss had turned her to a new way of living. This man, too, had known loss, for Peter had spoken often about his dead mother, his real mother, to her. Now as he began to talk she slowly realized that, although he had not withdrawn as she had, he had found his own way of enshrining the past and coping with the future.

"—and so, for Peter's sake, I married again, but my heart wasn't in things much. I began not to care. Let the bookshop go down. It was and still could be a good business. And then this memory thing of Peter's came to light."

"Memory thing?"

"Yes, it was something my wife discovered." He explained to her the circumstances and then went on, "She didn't encourage it . . . you know, to make him show off or anything. She didn't think it was right to do that. I'd almost forgotten about it until I was reading to him in bed one night before I remarried. I'd started a new book—some children's poems. I began to read a poem—" he laughed gently, "—I can remember it so clearly. Something he'd never heard before. Then after a few moments I saw he wasn't listening. Just staring out of the window. So I told him that he wasn't listening and he said he was and when I asked him what it was about he said he didn't know. He'd clearly been day-dreaming. But he asked what was the first line. So I gave it to him. '*A fair little girl sat under a tree, Sewing as long as her eyes could see . . .*' And then he just took it up and went right through to the point I'd reached in reading. That's how it all began. Don't ask me how he does it. He doesn't know himself. But that's all he needs. Then I got him to do it for a few friends and customers at the shop—and it all built up from there. Quite frankly it got to the point when I was exploiting him—for my own vanity, and the money. It wasn't all that much but it helped."

She sat listening as he went on and she knew that he was shriving himself. He explained how in the end he had met this Rundell man—who had been quite open with him and told him that he worked in the Foreign Office—and had gone to France with Peter. Everything came pouring out . . . the Comte de Servais' death and then the homecoming to find his wife in bed . . . And then just rejecting everything and running, taking Peter with him.

138

He finished. "I'm ringing Rundell in a few days' time to check when he will be in Plymouth and then I shall take Peter in and clear the whole thing up. Whatever Peter is carrying in his memory must be something highly secret and important, and Peter won't be safe until he's passed it on."

"But you can't think Peter's really in danger, can you?"

"Why not? The Count was murdered. Somebody in the Foreign Office passed the word for that. Somebody who knew. Like this Miss Lloyd or Rundell's assistant, Tampion, or whoever. God knows. But they were too late. All I know is that we're hiding out here, taking no chances, calling ourselves Grady instead of Courtney." His mouth twisted with disgust. "Pretty story, isn't it? And I just did it all for the cash—and right from the start my instinct was shouting to me that it was all risky. Fine kind of father for the boy, aren't I?"

"Yes, I would say that you don't come out of it well. But that's all passed. You're going to put it right. You're being honest with yourself now."

"Would you like us to leave the caravan?"

"Good Lord, why? Peter's safer here than anywhere else. You just stay until you've cleared everything with this Rundell."

"Thank you. I'm glad I told you. It's that much relief anyway."

"I'm glad you told me, too. And I know how hard it must have been. Now finish your brandy—and I'll keep you company with one, too."

After he and Peter had left, and Judy was abed in the spare room, Lady Diana went back and sat by the sitting-room fire, staring into the red embers and she thought—how easy it is to let oneself slip into the wrong ways, not just of acting but of thinking. Every word, action and emotion in the present inevitably shaped the future. And every loss left behind the seeding for new growth if you had the patience and willingness to nourish it. But so often it withered because one couldn't find the strength and courage to accept God's will and look to Him for some sign of guidance. In a different mood, as Courtney had talked, she could have despised him. But not now. The

139

loss of his Sarah had set him looking for any comfort ready at hand. What had she done after her loss? Much the same—nursed her grief, turned in on herself, and retired from her true world. Courtney had gone badly wrong—but something told her that he wouldn't stay wrong for long. And she—in a quite different way, she saw now—had gone wrong—let herself go, withdrawn, lost the habit of caring about herself. In another ten years they'd be calling her the witch of Hightop Farm. And the place would be a shambles. Just for tonight she had had to work like a dog to get dining-room and sitting-room back to some decent order. It was the first time, too, in years that she had given more than a passing thought to her appearance.

*   *   *   *

Lying in bed the next morning in the caravan and hearing his father stir on his bunk, Peter said, "Didn't you think Lady Diana looked super last night?"

"Yes, I did."

"You had a long time talking to her while we were in the kitchen. Did you get bored?"

"No, I didn't."

"What did you talk about?"

"Oh, lots of things. I told her about your memory thing. You don't mind?"

"No. Not her. But I wouldn't want anyone else down here knowing. Like Judy. She'd think I'm some sort of weirdo."

His father laughed. "You're far from that."

"Do you know what Judy said about her?"

"No."

"She said her young man got killed in the R.A.F. years ago and now she won't give any man the time of day."

"I don't think that's true—or kind."

"Neither do I. I mean about any other man. You know—" he yawned and stretched, "—since Joannie's no longer your wife, you'll have to think about getting another, won't you?"

"Why?"

"Well, who's going to do all the shopping, and the washing-

140

up, and looking after the laundry? You'll be at the shop and I'll be at school."

"Well, you've got a point there. Perhaps when we get back to London I'll think about it."

"Yes, I should. I think it's what we're going to need."

"What kind would you like? Tall, short, fat or thin, dark or fair haired, blue or brown eyes?"

"It isn't what I would like. It's what you would like."

"But if I left the choice to you, what would you like?"

"Oh, I don't know."

"What about Lady Diana?"

Peter laughed. "Some hope you've got there. She's Lady Diana Stormont. You'd have to have blue blood in your veins before you could even think about it."

"How do you know I haven't? My father always told me that we Courtneys came over with William the Conqueror and that one of them, Sir Gervais Courtney, much later on, was beheaded for making eyes at one of Henry the Eighth's wives. I forget which."

Peter laughed. "Pull the other one. When are we going to Plymouth to see Mr Rundell?"

"I'm going to telephone him today."

"Only Judy wants to know, so that if it's a weekday she can get to work on her mother to get to work on her father to make him write a note to school that she's too poorly to go that day. He's a bugger for her going to school regularly."

"I don't like that word much, Peter."

"Oh, it's all right down here. It's not a swear word with them. Mrs Preston says it sometimes. It's a sort of friendly word. I wouldn't use it anywhere else but down here." He laughed. "Could you imagine at school if some master asked me what date the Spanish Armada was and I said, 'Bugger if I know, sir'?"

He began to roll about on his bed laughing and his father laughed, too.

At that moment, Albert Horsfell, moving through the trees on the slope above the caravan, heard their laughter and thought how pleasantly the sound came through the early morning air. It was a sparkling, blue-skied day with the larks and meadow pipits singing, and the bloom on the thorn and everything in order in this best of possible worlds. And down the slope below the caravan his dismantled rifle, carefully wrapped in oil rags and waterproof sheeting, lay hidden under leaves in the heart of a rhododendron thicket. Tomorrow morning he would take up his position covering the path which Peter took to the bluff over the salmon pool, his car parked safely away on the hilltop road, false number plates on, and all traffic signals at Go. Lovely morning today. Let it be so tomorrow. But come rain or shine it would make no difference.

An hour later, more than usually hungry from his early morning call, he ate his breakfast with indiscriminate relish and read the London paper, which was on time. The headlines proclaimed some Government crisis and he shook his head sadly. Politicians—they were a useless lot. Well, over the years, he had done his little bit to remedy things by shooting two or three. *At home and abroad. Three languages like a native. Go anywhere—Do anything—Absolute discretion—Terms by no means moderate.* He smiled to himself as the waitress came to refill his coffee cup. It was one he hadn't seen before, but she had a run in her tights in exactly the same place as the other one. Coincidence, or did they share tights, or were they tights of the same make that always went in the left leg? Who knew? Life was full of teasing minor problems.

*   *   *   *

They walked down to Sleadon together in the evening and, instead of following the driveway across the meadow and down through the woods, Peter showed his father the shorter way he had found by taking the path to the salmon pool and then following the river track out on to the drive. It was a lovely evening with the sun low and reddening under the faint wash of a rising mist.

Peter said, "Will you be gone long?"

"No, not very. I'm going to walk up the hill to the telephone box on the main road."

"You could use Mr Preston's phone."

"I think not. This is all sort of private to you and me. You can have a chat with Judy while I'm gone. And don't forget to give Mrs Preston the list for our groceries."

"No, I won't. Will you know when you come back when we're going to Plymouth so I can tell Judy?"

"I should think so. Have you told her anything about it?"

"Oh, I just said we might be going again. But she was quite keen. She said Lady Diana's got a birthday soon and she wants to buy her a new cassette for her player. She likes old Beethoven stuff and that kind. Do you think we ought to buy her something?"

"Why not? She's been very nice to us. What do you suggest?"

"I don't know. A box of chocolates?"

"Why not? It's a safe enough bet. Unless we have to go on a Sunday."

"Oh, there'll be some shops open, down by the Barbican now all the holiday people are starting to come."

He left Peter at the cottage and walked up to the telephone box thinking—Soon now this whole business would be cleared up. And then a fresh start. Have the shop front re-painted. Reorganize it. Start again and make something out of it. The way he had first planned when Sarah was alive. Take over the flat. It was only on a monthly tenancy, furnished. Begin again. Funny, he'd been thinking lately that if Peter weren't so wedded to London they could have sold up the shop and opened up somewhere in the country ... somewhere down here. Tavistock or Plymouth. But he couldn't really see it. They were both Londoners. City sparrows. Still it was an idea.

He put his call through from the box and recognized Rundell's voice answering.

He said, "Mr Archibald here. Have you fixed the Plymouth thing?"

"Yes, I have. This coming Sunday. I shall be staying at the Holiday Inn. Will the afternoon, about three, suit you?"

"Yes, it will."

"Fine. We'll clear everything up. An end to the whole

business. How's your boy?"

"He's all right, thank you. See you on Sunday." He replaced the receiver.

*   *   *   *

Teddy Tampion, a glass of whisky at his side, on the floor alongside his armchair his open brief-case with the official papers he had been discussing with Rundell, cocked an eye at his chief and said, "Without being intrusive—Plymouth and the boy. Do I draw the right conclusions? The jolly old plot thickening, sir?"

Rundell laughed. "Indeed it is. In fact that's why I asked you to come round here. The opportune telephone call was a little serendipity."

"Horrid word."

"I agree. Words, like women, stand or fall on first impressions. One may be wrong about a woman, of course. But seldom over a word."

"So?"

"They are in the West Country. Courtney made contact with me. He wants everything off his chest. Wants to let the boy do his stuff, take his money and live happily ever after."

Tampion nodded. How easy life would be were it so, he thought. To live happily ever after, shaking off the embarrassing coils of deceit and discarding for ever more the need of stratagems and the compulsions of a twisted personality. But man is what he is and must live with it. He said, "Well, it will be good to know what the Comte de Servais said. Nice for us, I mean. But not for a lot of people. You will return with a rich argosy. If I may be allowed a touch of jolly old hyperbole."

Rundell sat down, took a cigar from the box at his side—refrained from offering Tampion one because he knew he never used them—and said, "The use of the word argosy is apt. As you know, many an argosy has foundered within sight of the home port. That's why I want you to come with me to this meeting with the boy and his father. If I went alone and taped the boy's message ... who knows what might happen?

A train crash on the way back, tape gone and a corpse with knowledge it can't communicate."

"We might both be on this ill-starred train."

"No. We travel separately. Those names on the Count's list have got to come back to London. So you come—make your own list of the names—and lengthen the already long odds by travelling without me."

"I see. And, of course, understand. Except for one thing. Why me and not Miss Lloyd? She ranks higher in your confidence than I, alas, do."

"How do you ever make a choice between two things or two people? By instinct? By ratiocination—another ghastly word. In my place what choice would you have made?"

"On the skimpy facts, very difficult. Assuming her name was on the list, and she knew or guessed it, she could have arranged it all. The original appointment with the Count, we know, was for the late afternoon. Then, he phones her in the early morning and changes things. Come to lunch and bring the boy. He'd be anxious to get things off his jolly old chest, anyway. Sooner shrived, sooner would peace come dropping slow, what? And she can do nothing to change the timings. We all know how slowly a feed-back like that can take to overcome the splendid bureaucratic block between communication and action... Oh, bless me—all this sounds unloyal. But you did ask, sir."

"And am listening with interest and an open mind. Now you? What is there to make me think that at some time, as the dagger goes in, I shall not turn and say, *Et tu, Tampion*?"

Tampion laughed. "None at all. I could just as easily have arranged it—and never even known that the Count would change the time of the appointment. I would have just sat in blissful, traitorous ignorance until the news came that your precious argosy had survived storm and wreck. And then have been glad that I had been given respite by Courtney taking off into the blue with his boy. Those are the two situations. Miss Lloyd's and mine. I'm glad the decision between us had to be yours. I won't ask you, sir, whether you made your decision on the limited facts or a prolonged study of some crystal ball."

Rundell laughed. "Neither. I simply tossed a coin and you won. You travel down and back separately."

Walking back across Hyde Park from Rundell's flat on his way to his club in Pall Mall, Tampion felt reasonably composed. But he was—and he told himself quite naturally—not entirely happy about things. One of the names on the list could turn out to be his. His cover had always been, he felt, impeccable. But impeccable in this jolly old slapdash world was not what it used to be. He could see himself in that hotel room while the little memory boy trotted out the list and his name came tripping off that innocent tongue. What then? One thing only—and that thing his ruthlessness so carefully concealed for years and years behind the Teddy Tampion mildly silly-ass manner—"But don't let that fool you, dear chap—he's as artful as a cageful of monkeys and as deep as the deepest well." Boy, father and Rundell—all would have to go. Three shots, and then an unhurried walk to the lift stairs while maybe someone in a near room said, "God, that sounded like shots." And some other someone keeping the first someone company, perhaps of an intimate nature, would say, "Don't be silly, darling—just a car back firing. Come on, darling, I've only got an hour before I have to meet boring old George." Yes, he could handle the possibility, but he would have to take some advice about it on his way home. *They* got most extraordinarily upstage if you took a step without consultation. Private initiative was frowned on. You might be doing the Devil's work but you still had to fill in the right forms first.

He left the Park at Hyde Park Corner and walked down under the trees to Buckingham Palace. For Queen and Country ... well, so it might have been if not for a young man's fancy lustfully turning to thoughts of love years ago. So, innocent and enchanted, Circe had taken him with her body ... An old, old story, and so hackneyed. Given herself and paid his mounting debts and little by little had made him theirs. Though he had to be fair and say that in the end the life style and the adrenalin thrust of the danger really suited him. At least life was no longer dull. Inside Teddy Tampion lay the other also alliterative persona of Michin Malicho. Room

146

mates for years.

From a booth inside his club he telephoned the Grayson Insurance Company.

He said, "Stormbird here . . ." Briefly he outlined his want and the reason for the need of it. When he had finished the voice at the other end said, "Hold on a minute, please caller." He held on. He knew the voices which answered him from time to time. Sometimes, wooing sleep at night, he tried to put sex and form to them. This was the woman with the pale grey voice, a little sad and soothing, motherly. And she proved all that this evening for when she came back she said, "I'm happy to tell you, Stormbird, that there won't be any need for it. Your little friend will never get to the meeting on Sunday. He's being taken care of by another department tomorrow morning."

"Permanently?"

"What else?"

"Well, that's a bonus."

"Yes . . . Perhaps you're a little relieved?"

"Well, I suppose you could say that, looking at it purely, my dear, from the point of view of one's work load. Nice to hear your voice again. Have you been on holiday?"

"Yes, you could call it that. I had a few weeks abroad, taking my dear mother to the sun. Goodbye."

Light-stepped and light-hearted, after all it was a bonus to find that someone else was going to do your work for you, he went to the bar and said, "A large Haig, Harry. How's your jolly old missus, over her 'flu?"

"Yes, she is, sir. Back to her old form, and back-handing me if I step out of line. Bless her dear old heart."

CHAPTER TEN

ALBERT HORSFELLL TOOK an early breakfast. The day, he was glad to see, was a fine one. He ate with a good, sharp appetite. There had been times in the distant past when, a tyro in his profession, he had known the equivalent of stage nerves, the tension and butterflies in the stomach which long preceded action. Many a breakfast in those days had gone scarcely touched by him. But now he was an old hand and had himself well schooled. With completely detached professionalism he considered the morning hours ahead of him.

Finish breakfast, and pay the bill—his case already packed and waiting in the hall—and then the not too long drive out to Sleadon. He had found a better parking place than at the gate by the footpath across the meadow to the caravan. Half-way back down the hill there was an old lay-by where the local council dumped gravel and stones for road repairs. There was plenty of room for him to park and he could walk through the trees, across the old driveway, and then through more trees until he reached his chosen spot. In the lay-by he would change the car's number plates (false) for another set (false). Double, double saved toil and trouble. Today was Friday when the boy went down around ten-thirty to collect the basket of groceries brought by the roundsman. The little path ran within fifteen yards of the great clump of rhododendron bushes in which his rifle now lay hidden. In his imagination he saw the boy passing ... whistling like a bird on his way down to the bluff overlooking the river pool. He would give him fifty yards ... the boy whistling, the brawling stream that came down from the caravan site making its bright chatter. One shot would do it and then he would be away while the echoes

aded among the trees. And within three hours he would have
out more than a hundred miles between himself and Sleadon.
There had been a time, long ago, when he would have been
curious about what lay behind this assignment. After all man
was a curious beast, questions rising in his mind like smoke
from a fire ... curiosity, perhaps, one of the mainsprings of
evolution. The first man who rubbed two sticks together out of
boredom, replete with full stomach, idle, content, just rubbing
and then noticing that the friction made one of the sticks warm
and then hot ... Now, he had no curiosity. Not his to question
why.

He left a good tip for the waitress, a very good tip, and wondered whether she would treat herself to a new pair of tights.
The clerk in the reception office hoped he had had a pleasant
stay and, in reply to his question, gave him directions for
finding the road west to Cornwall and Falmouth, directions to
which he scarcely listened because he was going back to
London, though he had been to Falmouth once, long ago ...
something to do with one of the crew of a Russian fishing boat.
Nice little town with, in the season, the smell of Cornish
pasties heavy and redolent everywhere.

He drove off and some way out of the town was surprised
and pleased to see a sparrowhawk come winging over the road
hedge, swift and silent as a corsair, and take a wren from a
thorn tip with hardly a falter in flight. A beautiful sight ...
every God-endowed instinct and muscle combining faultlessly
in the act. Dear, dear, he mustn't start thinking about God.
Suffer little children to come unto Me. Not a sparrow falls ...

He drove, whistling reedily and low to himself. Just over an
hour later he was installed in his rhododendron clump, his rifle
assembled. On any other day, he thought, it would have been
an ideal hide for bird-watching, but now his true professionalism swamped everything. A Dartford warbler, a rara avis, he
thought, could have perched on the tip of the rifle barrel and
left him unmoved. Never at the moment of professional con-
centration let the mind wander to the contemplation of
amateur delights.

Peter, combing his hair in the small caravan mirror, making

himself ready to go down to the Prestons said to his father "Do you think I should run up to Lady Diana's and ask her i there's anything she wants? I'll be down there before the van comes and he always carries a lot of extra stuff in case people want it."

"Well, it would be a kindness, wouldn't it?"

"Do you want more cigarettes?"

"No, I'm all right."

Peter looking at himself in the glass said, "I'm getting sunbrowned, you know."

"So you are—a regular darky."

His big shopping basket over his arm, Peter walked up the short length of driveway to Hightop Farm and found Lady Diana in the small paddock throwing out corn for her hens. When he asked her if she needed anything from the van she said, "I don't think so, thank you, Peter." She paused for a moment and then giving him a smile, went on, "But there is something I would like sometime."

"Oh, what's that?"

"Well, when you and your father were up here to dinner he told me about your memory thing. Did he tell you?"

"Yes, he did."

"Would you like to do it for me some time?"

"Well ..." he hesitated. "Well ... I was sort of thinking I didn't ever want to do it again. You know, it's a freaky sort of thing. I never told any of the chaps at school about it."

"Oh, I don't know. God gives different people different gifts. Some can play the piano by ear and not know a note of written music. Others can draw and paint things marvellously from childhood. If He gives you something which makes you a little special, well ... it would be ungrateful not to be glad about it. After all, He doesn't do anything without a purpose, does He?"

"I suppose not. But I wish He'd given me ... well, playing music or drawing. That's not so freakish. Still, I see what you mean. And, of course, if you want me to some time I will."

"That's nice of you. Perhaps we will some time."

"O.K. Do you like poetry?"

"Yes, a lot. Don't you?"

"Not much, really. You sure that you don't want anything?"

"Sure."

"Then I'll be off . . ." he paused and then added with a grin, 'Your Ladyship."

Smiling, she watched him move away. Then with a small sigh she thought, God gives and God takes. She could have married, had His will been different, and had children. A boy like Peter. Then feeling the rise of a mood of self-pity she turned away and went on feeding the hens. After the chore was done she went into the house, poured herself a glass of sherry and reached for her cigarettes . . . small consolations.

* * * *

Albert Horsfell heard the boy coming down the hill behind him, the sound of his whistling rising above the music of the tumbling stream on the far side of the rhododendron clump. Let him, he thought, pass and go down to the bluff. And for the first time, surprising him, he felt the rise of an edge of self-disgust. He had known it before, years ago, and had long thought it conquered. And conquered—not difficult because it had little force—it had to be now. Work was work, and a man could not live without wages—whether they came from virtues or sins. Dear, oh dear . . . what a stupid and irritating twinge of conscience—fated though to die almost before it showed the first signs of life.

The boy came by, ten yards away on the rough path, swinging his basket, wind-breaker open, the bottom of his jeans rolled up, his feet bare of stockings in his open-work sandals. He passed by. Horsfell let him go. A moving target you had to take if you knew you weren't going to get a standing one. But he knew that he was going to get a standing one because the boy's movements were almost always the same. He would go down on to the bluff and stand looking into the water for a while, motionless, watching the fish or just the run of the current. That was the moment to take him for with luck he

151

would go over into the river and, with more luck, it could b
hours, maybe a day, before he was found. No one but a foo
would ignore the bonus of time in a getaway.

Lying full length, he settled the rifle comfortably in positio
and covered the boy as he moved. The boy stopped at th
bottom of the path and bent to pick up a few stones. Rhythn
and ritual, thought Horsfell—how much they governed ou
lives. He had seen the lad do it every time. A few stones to tos
over into the river, probably to disturb the fish and see then
flash away to their hiding places. Well, he would grant him th
grace of that last pleasure. After the stones were gone he woul
take him. He lay there covering the boy, watching the side
ways flick of one hand as the stones were tossed into the river
Then, with the last stone gone, the boy stood motionless
watching the river pool.

He took him in his sights, finger on the trigger, breathec
deeply and then let his lungs slowly empty so that he woulc
come to a point of complete immobility. A cold ecstasy wen
through him, freezing all thought and emotion and his fore
finger met the trigger with the softest of caresses, waiting fo
the boy to turn . . . seeing now the beginning of that movemen
inhabit the young body.

Behind him, with a steely, yet muted harshness, a woman'
voice, not to be mistaken even in this moment of tenseness
said quietly, "You do that and I blow your head off!"

He made no move to turn or take away his trigger finger. I
almost a whisper the voice said, "Put the rifle away to you
side and then stay as you are until the boy moves away."

He put the rifle to his side, his eyes still on the boy, but hi
mind on the author of this inappropriate intervention. He wa
no fool. While you lived the gods of chance might give som
reprieve. The boy moved away from the bluff upstream, dawd
ling and swinging his basket, and finally disappeared alon
the narrow woodland track. He lived an age waiting for th
voice to come again. Somewhere in the high trees he heard a
chiff-chaff calling and up a frond of the winter-sear clump o
trampled grass before him a ladybird laboriously made it
black-and-red-dominoed way to nowhere in particular. Prid

is nothing, he thought, in the survival stakes. Under threat he could be humble. The great thing was to survive. Where there was life there was hope. He could be humble and wait with the best of them. But never forget that the gods help them who help themselves. Any of the gods would do. In his state he was not particular.

The voice said, "Stand up slowly and keep your back to me."

It was a good voice, educated, cultured, no farm woman. It had a background—his mind was going like a dynamo under full load—of breeding, a tone which any servant in good service would recognize at once. He rose on his hands and knees, man-ape seeking to throw the load of his past from his shoulders so that he could stand straight and look with ease into the sky and begin true worship. And a brighter future.

As he moved, bearing on his open hands, he dug at the loose mould and soil and gripped the primitive, the only survival means at his command. But when he was on his feet, upright, he turned quickly and flung his handfuls of dirt, small stones and dead leaves at the woman who stood a few feet from him.

Surprised, she stumbled back, gave a little cry and then began to raise the shotgun she carried. He turned and ran, swinging round the rhododendron clump and heading uphill through the trees towards the old drive, his shoulders hunched as he waited for the blast and sting of gunshot. He reached a great oak trunk six feet beyond the rhododendrons and slipped behind it as the shot came and whistled by the tree and smacked into its tough bark. He ran on, untouched, putting trees and bushes between him and the woman and when she fired again he heard the shots go wide to his right and guessed why. Her surprise and her haste were serving him, not her.

He ran then and the feeling rose strong in him that although the day had gone wrong, it was yet his day. There was no sound of pursuit, no more gunfire. He accepted the grace the gods had given him without curiosity.

He came to the old driveway, ran across it, jumped the small stream on the far side and went on through the trees until he reached the hill road some yards below the lay-by.

153

He got into the car and drove off in the direction he was facing and he knew that for the time being—for shock was strong in him now, and disgust that pure chance had brought him ill luck—he would just drive until his mind was settled. When it had, he stopped and checked his bearings and found that he had been going north. Consulting his map he decided to drive on northwards and stay the night at Barnstaple, abandon his car there, and take the train to London the next day. Late that afternoon he parked his car in the town centre car park where for all he cared it could moulder away to eternity. Case in hand he walked to a riverside hotel, booked a room, ordered a large whisky and drank it while he bathed. Failure came hard to him, but what, he thought, could a man do when for once his luck ran out? *They* wouldn't like it when he telephoned to announce his failure. Well, too bad ... the best laid plans of mice and men ... He dressed, putting on a different suit, and started down the stairs first for the telephone booth to report to his employers and then on to the bar to ease his still strong professional chagrin at his failure with a large whisky.

A little way down the broad stairs he tripped on a recent tear in the carpet and fell the length of more than half the flight, striking his head on the bannister pillar at the bottom of the stairs and sliding across the polished reception hall floor to come to rest in a heap at the feet of an elderly lady who was sitting on a settee, doing the *Daily Telegraph* crossword, who for a while thought he was drunk and proceeded to tell him so.

He was admitted to hospital half an hour later, suffering from concussion and a broken leg, and remained concussed for two days.

*   *   *   *

Lady Diana had picked up the rifle and taken it back to Hightop Farm with her. It was only by the grace of God that she had gone down into the woods. A few minutes after Peter had left that morning she had found that what she had thought was a full—and her last—packet of cigarettes was empty. She

154

didn't smoke much but she liked the odd one now and again. So she had gone after Peter to ask him to bring her some from the delivery van, knowing that she would easily catch him because he always loitered for a while at the salmon pool. As always she took her shotgun with her on the chance of getting a pigeon or rabbit for the pot. Thank God she had.

Even now the distress and shock lingered in her. She had walked on down to the Preston's cottage and found him there, with the van just arrived. There had been no question of her saying anything to him—or even to his father at this stage. The man who had run from her wasn't likely to come back, she reasoned. He would think she had already put the police on to him.

But what was she to do? That question had stayed with her all day. She had the rifle, which she had hidden before going down to the Preston's house, and had recovered after she had seen Peter safely back to the caravan.

Now, here was evening and she hadn't yet the faintest idea what she ought to do. Her first thought had been to tell the father—but she turned against that quickly. He already had enough on his plate and was only looking forward to Sunday when he could get the whole business cleared up so that he could go back to London and start his life all over again.

Common-sense told her that the attempt on the boy's life almost certainly must be connected with his trip to France. And it followed logically enough what his father had long suspected, had known almost when he first agreed to take the boy there, that this Comte de Servais had passed no ordinary information to the boy. My God ... what a damn fool of a man. Like him as she did she had to admit that he must have wanted his head examined for agreeing to it. But then who was perfect? She'd been a damned fool in a different way. Shutting herself away with her grief. It was easier to blame people than to understand them. What one did out of grief, greed or desperation you could make seem right at the time. But time itself soon undeceived you. His Sarah must have known that. She it was almost certainly who had held things together. One thing had through the passing hours become quite clear to her. She had to have advice, and advice from a source utterly to be trusted, and one which was part of the world in which Rundell, the Comte de Servais and all the others lived. Utterly to be trusted was the main point. And who in this world could lay claim to that virtue? Well, maybe no one absolutely. Well, there was no living in this world without accepting that.

She got up and walked to the sitting-room window and looked out. The sun had gone below the horizon and the western sky was a fading red glow. Down the drive father and son were probably eating their supper in the caravan. The father waiting for Sunday and freedom to begin all over again, and the boy as innocent as an angel.

Suddenly she turned on her heels and went to the telephone, consulted her telephone pad and then dialled a London number. When it was answered she said, "I'd like to speak to Lady Endsworth, please. Will you tell her that it is Diana speaking."

She waited for a few moments and then a woman's voice said happily from the other end, "Diana! My darling, don't tell me you're in London?"

"No, Pat, love, I'm not. Still living on my hilltop and casting spells."

"It's time you tried one on yourself and came out into the light. Why don't you come up and stay with us? We'd so love to have you. It's been ages."

"I know. Perhaps I will soon." As she spoke she was thinking that she had only been up there twice since it had all happened ... all those years ago.

"You should make it sooner than soon, my love. Still, it's no good my arguing with you except that as Jimmy's mother I can say that he would never have wanted you to shut yourself away from the world. However, no more badgering. What can I do for you?"

"I don't suppose that Richard is in at the moment, is he?"

"No, he's not. He's at Westminster explaining to his fellow Lordships how the only way to maintain peace in this wicked world is to arm ourselves to the teeth. I sometimes wonder about it myself. But there you are, Richard's all for put your

156

trust in God and keep your armour bright."

"Do you think he would be kind enough to give me a call when he gets back? No matter how late?"

"I'm sure he would. Was there ever a time when he wouldn't do anything for you? Oh, did you hear that Pat Hansford was getting divorced ... silly girl. Everyone told her. It stuck out like a sore thumb..."

Listening as Lady Endsworth ran on, she smiled to herself. She was the greatest rattler of gossip in all time—except when it came to anything to do with her husband. And then she was a clam.

When she had finished with the telephone call she went into the sitting-room, threw a handful of small kindling on the fire to revive it, then poured herself a glass of sherry and sat in thought as the blue and yellow flames began to lick and grow around the dry wood. Dear Pat was right, of course. You couldn't stay for ever, hidden away from the world, licking your wounds and hugging your sorrows. The trouble was that you could know it was wrong and still not have the volition to take action. That she realized had to come from outside. And for days now she had been feeling the change working in her— ever since, in fact, she had first met Frank Courtney and Peter. Peter it was who had stirred her emotions. Had she and Jimmy married they could well have had a boy of the same age now ... and now here was this boy, strangely gifted, appealing, and walking unknown to himself along the dark and dangerous paths of a world full of deceit and violence. It was odd and inexplicable, but there was no denying the slow growth of change in her, and that growth accelerated now by the morning's event. She could still see Peter, standing above the pool, and that swine of a man lying full stretch and the rifle being raised to mark him ... She shivered, and when she reached for her glass, her hand shook so that she spilled the sherry.

It was just after ten o'clock when Lord Endsworth came through. After a few pleasantries, she put her problem and her request to him.

After a long pause, he said, "Yes, naturally I do know all

about it. But you're asking me to do something which, if I had any, would make my hair stand on end. Also it means going behind the backs of a lot of people who could martyr me if things go wrong."

She said gently, "We nearly had a martyr down here this morning. I want the boy right out of this. All you have to do is to give me what I want and then make whatever arrangements you feel necessary at your end. But I must have what I want tonight."

"My dear Diana—you really are asking a great deal of me."

"Yes, I know." She paused, hearing his breathing at the far end of the line and, before he could speak, went on, "If Jimmy could be in your place he would have done it."

Lord Endsworth sighed. "*Touché*. All right." He laughed suddenly. "I'll put my head on the block for you. I'll ring you back later. Dear, dear, and I was just going to put my feet up with a large whisky and a few chapters of Boswell in the Hebrides with Dr Johnson. I'd left them on Rasay where the dear Doctor was being most uncomplaining at the lack of proper toilet facilities in the Laird's house."

An hour later the telephone rang again for her.

At almost the same time the telephone rang in Tampion's flat. The subsequent conversation was brief.

A woman's voice said, "Recently, we turned down a request from you for life insurance. But it appears there was some misunderstanding. I won't go into it except to say that we agree to the cover you asked for. Will you pick up the necessary forms tomorrow from our local agent before you leave on your business trip?"

"Yes, certainly."

Tampion put the receiver back and took a deep breath. He could fill in the unspoken details. Some idiot in the field had bungled things. He was now on his own again. If his name came out of the hat on Sunday the boy, his father and Rundell would have to go and he himself move to some distant sanctuary. Three shots. Maybe four to be certain. But usually they just stood, wondering why the world was suddenly revolving backwards. Rundell first because he might be armed, then the boy, and then the father who would be wondering if he could believe his eyes.

*   *   *   *

Saturday morning. A light drizzle had fallen earlier. The flag, hoisted by Peter when he had gone out to get their washing water from the stream, hung limply against the masthead. The caravan was redolent with the aromas of eggs and bacon and coffee as they ate breakfast.

Peter said, "I hope it's not like this tomorrow. Have you looked up the times of the bus?"

"Yes. Don't fuss."

"Well, I do a bit. Judy wanted it to be Saturday so she could do a lot of shopping. Now her mother's said since she can't do much she can go and pay a call on an aunt they've got there after lunch. I won't tell you what she said about that. But she's going, anyway."

"You're not worried about saying your bit for Mr Rundell, are you?"

"No, of course not. Not about that."

"What about, if anything?"

"Well, about doing it any more. We aren't going to, are we?"

"No, I've promised you."

Peter laughed. "Cut your throat and may I die?"

Courtney laughed. "Absolutely. This will be positively your farewell performance."

"Oh, well, I don't mind doing it for a lark sometimes at a party. You know, friends, if you'd like that."

"No, I don't think so. One last performance and you retire. You know—you could get a job as a cook anywhere. How'd you get the bacon so crispy?"

Peter laughed. "Secret. You're an awful cook, aren't you?"

"Yes. And I'm staying that way. It saves me a lot of hard work." He reached forward and softly punched his son on the cheek. Tomorrow it would all be finished. London again, and a new beginning. He said, "What are you going to do today?"

"Well, I'm going up for the milk to Lady Diana's, and she said she'd put me up on that old pony of hers and teach me to ride ... well, begin to."

His father laughed. "Put a towel down the back of your pants."

"That's an idea. Mum used to ride, didn't she?"

"Yes—like the wind. It used to scare me stiff. I can't stand the things."

Peter was thoughtfully silent for a moment and then said, "Yes. I can see that. You're not really a country one, are you?"

"No—not if you mean full-time."

"Nor me. But just now and again is all right."

After Peter had gone up to Hightop Farm, Frank Courtney tidied up the caravan and made up the bunk beds. As he worked he thought that while he did not like the countryside all that much he had to admit that it was a good place for hauling yourself away to. Nothing much happened and a man had time to sit and think. And he had done a lot of thinking ... about himself. And about the future. He would make the shop over. There was a good living in the shop. Better than he had ever made so far because he had just let it drift. Antiquarian and secondhand books—he loved them and once had been a great reader. Funny how that had gone when Sarah had died. Take possession of the flat. Do it over. Get a woman to come in and clean. Marry again? He doubted it. But one never knew ... By God, one never knew about a lot of things.

*   *   *   *

Peter fell off once, although the old pony was doing little more than ambling over the rough pasture. But, although when they had finished he felt as though his stomach had been jolted upside down, he enjoyed himself. After that he picked up the hens' eggs from the outbuildings. They laid all over the place. And then went into the kitchen for a glass of milk and biscuits with Lady Diana.

As he sat down on the hardwood chair she cocked an eye at him and said, "Would you like a cushion for your bottom?"

160

He laughed. "Not really. I suppose you get used to it if you do it enough?"

"That's true."

She was silent for a while then she said, "Peter?"

"Yes, ma'am?"

"Do you like me?"

He laughed. "What a question! Of course I do. I think you're super. You know, you make things fun. Like my mother used to."

"You loved her very much, didn't you?"

"Of course."

She grinned. "Do you love me?"

"Well... Yes. In a way. I mean ... well, not like my mother."

"Of course not. Mothers are special. But if you love me—will you do something for me?"

"Yes, of course I will—though I hope it's not to muck out the pig's sty."

"No, it's nothing like that. It's your memory thing."

"Oh, that."

"You said you would do it some time for me."

"Yes, I know. But Dad's agreed that once we go back to London I shan't do it any more. It's a sort of freakish thing and I don't care for it."

"Well, it's something God gave you so it can't be a bad freakish thing, can it? Will you do it just for me? I'll give you something your father told me that he gave you a long time ago. Does that make any difference that it is a long time ago?"

"No. You want me to do it right now, sitting at the table?"

"If you would."

"O.K. Just give me a few moments." He leant forward, the habit still strong in him from the past, and leant his head on his arms. That bit meant nothing to him. It was all part of the act. But it made it seem a bit special to people. She was a nice lady, he thought. Her father had been a lord and her boy friend who was killed in the R.A.F.—so Judy had told him—had been the son of a lord.

He raised his head and smiled at her.

"Ready?"

"Yes."

"Here it is then." She quoted—"'*A fair little girl sat under a tree, Sewing as long as her eyes could see—*'." Then she stopped.

For a moment Peter hesitated and then took up the poem.

> "*Then smoothed her work and folded it right,*
> *And said, 'Dear work, good night! good night!'*
> *Such a number of rooks came over her head,*
> *Crying 'Caw! caw!' on their way to bed;*
> *She said as she watched their curious flight,*
> *'Little black things, good night! good night!'*'"

He went on right through the poem and when he finished she said, "Why, Peter—that's marvellous."

He shrugged his shoulders and grinned. "I think it's a pretty soppy sort of poem."

"You do? Well, it was written by a lord."

"Was it?" It seemed to him, and he grinned slightly, that there were a lot of lords about this morning.

Lady Diana smiled and said, "If you do one more I'll let you have three shots with my four-ten before you go back to the caravan. But only on one condition—that you don't tell your father about any of this."

"Of course not. But why?"

"You can keep a secret, can't you?"

"Well, yes—I suppose so. But it depends . . ."

" . . . I know. On whether it's a good or a bad secret to keep. Well this would be a good secret to keep. I want to help your father very much. I like him a lot you know—and this would be helping him. You would want to help him wouldn't you? Say he was in trouble?"

Peter laughed. "He is. When we came back from France he found out he wasn't really married. And there are other things too."

"Yes, he told me about some of them. But I want us to do something that will be an absolute secret between us because it's not something he can do for himself. Does that sound a bit muddled?"

"Yes. But if you really can help my father then, of course, I'd do anything you say."

"Cross your heart and hope to die?"

"Yes."

"All right then. You make yourself ready and I'll give you the beginning of something you've done before, like the first one. Ready?"

"Give me a few moments." He leaned forward again and rested his face in his arms. He was thinking that he didn't really understand all this but if Lady Diana wanted to help his father he was ready to do anything. But he couldn't see for the life of him what help his father wanted now that Mr Rundell was coming to Plymouth. But then you never knew with grown-ups. They kept a lot of things to themselves. Like his mother used to say—'People are like icebergs. One third showing and two thirds hidden. Only the blessed saints see them whole.' She really was a sharp one and funny with it, too. Lady Diana was as different as chalk from cheese from her.

He rested his head in his arms for a while. Then he sat back in his chair, gave her a big grin, and said, "I'm ready, your Ladyship."

"Here we are then."

With a pronunciation which would have pleased her long-dead governess, she said, "Il était une fois un Grand Ours qui vivait en Orient et qui avait un tas d'enfants. Quand ceux-ci grandirent ils s'en allèrent gagner leur vie dans différents pays."

When she stopped Peter was silent for a moment or two and, still keeping his head down, resting in his cupped hnds, he began, "De temps en temps ils envoyaient à leur père des nouvelles . . ."

He went on quoting, finally giving the full list of the names which the Comte de Servais had spoken.

As he finished and sat back in his chair Lady Diana said, "That's marvellous!"

"Oh, I don't know. It's nothing really to do with me."

"You may not think so, but it is. When people are born God

163

gives them gifts. He gave you that one. Just as He gives some people the gift to compose great music, or to become famous athletes and sportsmen."

"I'd rather have had that. I'm hopeless at cricket or football. Where did you get all that French stuff from?"

Calmly she said, "Why, from Mr Rundell. He's a friend of mine. He wanted me to give you a rehearsal for tomorrow ... you know, like actors do. And also asked me if you would do him a favour tomorrow. It's only a small one."

"What favour?"

She explained to him and when she had finished he said, puzzled, "Just that? Is that all?"

"Yes, just that."

"Well, of course—if that's what he wants. But I don't understand really."

"I know. But then take soldiers. Their officers give them orders to do things in war and they don't understand the why or the wherefore of the order. But they obey their officers without question." She grinned. "'Into the valley of death rode the six hundred'."

Peter laughed. "And a fat lot of good that did them. Now can I have my go with the four-ten, please?"

"Of course. Let's find some old tin cans, shall we?"

That evening Teddy Tampion and Mr Rundell—who had travelled separately by car and train—had dinner together in their hotel, dining off excellent grilled sole and sharing a bottle of Chablis. As they were taking their coffee together in the lounge a waiter told Mr Rundell that he was wanted on the telephone. When he had gone to answer it Tampion lit a cigar and prepared to enjoy it with his large brandy. A man might not know what the future held for him, but optimism and a tight contingent plan were always comforting. Poor old Rundell ... the bloody office never gave him a moment's peace ... the price one paid for high appointment.

On the telephone Rundell had the briefest of conversations.

"Rundell here."

A woman's voice said, "The answer to your two questions is *Yes* and *Yes*."

"Thank you."

He went to the reception desk and gave his order for a morning call at eight with grapefruit and a copy of *The Sunday Times*. He then went back to Tampion and said, "That was Courtney. He and the boy will be here at three o'clock." Then as he sat down, he cocked an eye at Tampion and said, "I don't suppose you'd care to come to church with me tomorrow morning?"

"That's very kind of you. But I think I shall go for a stroll on the Hoe and fill my London-starved lungs with some jolly old ozone. My immortal soul is beyond help."

CHAPTER ELEVEN

THEY WERE UP early on Sunday morning. The day was bright with a fresh wind blowing so that their caravan flag whipped and curled as though it were some strange great bird seeking to escape from a snare. Thinking that, Frank Courtney felt that this day, thank God, he and the boy would be freeing themselves from a trap of his own making. He had been a greedy, self-pitying fool. But after today that would all be behind. The future would be theirs to shape the way they wanted it.

After breakfast they washed up and tidied the caravan. He smiled to himself as they worked. Peter had become a great one for keeping things tidy.

He said, "You should be a sailor. They're great ones for keeping everything ship-shape and Bristol fashion."

"Well, I don't like things in a muddle."

And neither did he, not now anyway. Today was going to see the end of all their muddles.

Lady Diana came for them in her Land-Rover. She had insisted that she should drive them into Tavistock to catch the coach, picking Judy up at the Prestons' cottage on the way.

Looking at her, Peter was surprised to see someone almost foreign to him. She was wearing a grey coat and skirt, a red blouse with a pearl brooch at the neck, silk stockings and highly polished brown shoes. Perched on her head as though at any moment it might sprout wings and fly off was a fancy little straw hat with a small bunch of woodcock feathers sewn into its band.

Peter said, "Gosh—you're all dressed up, too. Are you going somewhere special?"

She laughed. "Well, in a way I am. After I've dropped you I'm going to church in Tavistock. I haven't been for years."

"Why not? Dad and I go most Sundays at home." He made a face. "Sometimes early Mass."

His father, catching the moment of embarrassment in her, said, "Peter—you and your questions."

Lady Diana chuckled. "Why shouldn't he ask? I don't mind." She touched Peter's cheek with the back of her hand gently. "The fact is that I've decided to turn over a new leaf. To stop living like a hermit up here. Or should I say hermitress? Never mind." There was the faintest touch of nervousness in her voice. "I just want to tell God about it and ask for his help."

"You mean you won't go on living up here?"

"Oh, yes. But I shall get out and around more. Go and see all my old friends in London and so on..."

"Oh, that's good. You can come and see us at the book shop. And I'll show you round places, if you like."

"Yes, I would. Now come on, we don't want to miss that coach, do we?" Over Peter's head she caught his father's eyes and saw that he was smiling, a smile she had never seen on his face before, as though in him some warm and tender emotion had wakened from a long sleep. In that moment she had a sharp, intense longing for a sensation which she had not known for years—the feeling of a man's arms around her, of the security and comfort of being enfolded and protected. Oddly, too, she felt that this man was aware of her feeling...

They drove down the bumpy old driveway to Sleadon where Judy was waiting at the cottage garden gate. She was dressed up, too, in a blue dress with a light grey flannel summer coat and a funny sort of hat, Peter thought, shaped like an acorn cup inside down. As he sat in the back of the Land Rover with her on the way to Tavistock, Peter said, "You don't look like you."

"I don't feel like me. But Mum said no daughter of hers was going to Aunt Tilly looking like three-pennyworth of nothing. I got a lecture too—about the way I talk. None of that buggering. Aunt Tilly's Methodist and very strict. Dad says that when Uncle Wilf died she must have missed him dreadful. Not having anyone to bully and tell to take his muddy shoes off before he came in, and making him go in the garden if he wanted a smoke."

Peter grinned. "It looks like you're going to enjoy yourself."

"I would if Uncle Wilf was still alive. He used to be a gardener down at the big house before it all broke up. And on the side Dad says he was the cleverest poacher for miles around here." She leaned towards him and whispered in his ear, "I ain't never seen her Ladyship dressed like that before. I think she could be keen on your Dad."

"Don't be daft. She's a Lady."

She giggled softly and whispered, "That don't matter a bugger when it comes to love."

That morning Mr Rundell went to church and was pleased that two of the hymns were favourites of his so that he could let himself go. The sermon, he thought, lacked coherence and gave him nothing to bite on. Which was as well, perhaps, because it allowed his thoughts to dwell on the coming afternoon and the extraordinary diversity of human natures and how life altered people. Small events bringing great changes. There's a destiny that shapes our ends rough-hew them how we may ... Dear, dear, how far away now was that small prep. schoolboy Eric Rundell who had once dreamed in a freezing dormitory of going to Kenya and being a tea-planter like his Uncle and being warm all the time. Not that he cared for tea much.

And Edward Tampion walking on the Hoe stopped at the war memorial, which towered high above him and thought wryly *Dulce est pro patria mori* ... yes, why not? If that was the way you thought about it. But Drake, whose memorial, too, was close by, and who had finished his game of bowls here before going out to beat the Spaniards with their Armada had been a rough-tongued, free-booting old pirate and had long lain fathoms deep off Portobello. Men had two sides. God's and the Devil's and—overlooking the workings of Destiny—believed they had a free choice to make between them. Not so. The fall of a leaf or a pin could change a man's destiny. There jolly well, old boy, was no getting away from that. How could that poor little sod of a boy ever dream of what this day might bring forth...?

To take up time before they had lunch the three of them walked to their hotel by way of the Barbican and up around by the Citadel. Quite a few shops were open and Judy found a little model of Drake's *Golden Hind* for her aunt, saying, "I daren't tell her I bought it on a Sunday. But she'll like it. Give her something else to dust. She always has a duster in her hand."

And Frank Courtney, with them, but not with them, hearing their chatter, felt a slow ease fill him because this day had to bring an end to their troubles and the beginning of a new life. God had punished him because of his vanity over the boy's strange gift ... and he had learnt his lesson. Sarah had said once, 'What Man does to Man, the Holy Mother is not all that concerned with. But abuse a child and there's no saving you from the rough side of Her tongue.' Sarah. As different as she could have been from Lady Diana... Never mixed up as this one was. Though he had the feeling that she was coming out of it. Dressed up today. A fine woman. What had brought that about? He didn't know for sure, but he had an idea that it might well be something to do with their being in the caravan. Not him. But Peter. Well, if she had decided to come out of her sorrowing it could only be for the good. He had known such a moment after Sarah had gone. You couldn't go on coddling your grief for ever. The world was there always, waiting for you.

They went to the hotel at the far end of the Hoe where they had lunched before, and they got a window seat so that they could look out to sea.

He ate little himself but both the children did full justice to the menu. Judy told some country stories in dialect which made them laugh and, even in his preoccupation with the coming afternoon, he noticed that she was schooling her language and being a proper young lady. Peter he could see was thoroughly enjoying himself and eating everything within sight. There clearly was no nervousness in him about the afternoon's coming demonstration. God ... he would be glad to have it all over.

Rundell and Tampion had lunch together and after it was over Rundell said, "I shall go up and have a little shut-eye, my dear Tampion. An old doctor friend of mine used to say that even fifteen minutes flat after eating could put years on your life."

As he went Tampion thought ... well, yes, barring one of life's little accidents.

*   *   *   *

After a lengthy lunch Judy went off reluctantly to see her aunt and Peter and his father walked down to the Holiday Inn. They asked at the desk for Mr Rundell and after a little while Edward Tampion came down to them.

He gave Peter a big grin and said, "Well, here we are then, what? The return of the jolly old prodigals, what? Come on I'll take you up to the Big Chief himself."

Curious, he thought, as he led the way to the lift—his automatic lying flat and neat in his jacket pocket, undisturbing the flawlessness of its cut—how you could like someone and yet know that it would not make a hair's breadth of difference in the action that might be forced on you. Survival was all. Sentiment mustn't be allowed to clog the smooth running machine for a second. If things went against him, his car was waiting just around the corner. Drive five miles and someone would be waiting for him in another car. Sell your soul to the Devil, he thought, and you got service of the highest order.

Peter said, "I like lifts. That sort of soft bump as they take off and stop."

"Simple pleasures, my old dear—the best in life." He turned to Frank Courtney. "You both look brown and fit. Have you had a good time?"

"Yes. We've been enjoying ourselves. Is it just going to be you and Mr Rundell?"

"That's it. A jolly foursome. Then, if you wish, you can take the next train back to London. Might have to wait a bit—" he

170

winked at Peter,"—Sunday service, you know."

Peter said, "We're not going back just yet, sir."

"And why should you—keep away from the hustle and bustle."

Mr Rundell was waiting for them and he shook hands with both of them. As they sat down he said to Peter, "Now wasn't it a lucky thing I happened to be coming to Plymouth with Mr Tampion and we found out about your being down here? So, what did I think? I thought—I wonder if that boy has as good a memory as I fancy he has."

"I don't know, sir."

"Well, we'll have to see. You don't mind if I put the tape recorder on while you do it, do you?"

"No, sir."

Mr Rundell reached out, switched on the tape recorder which stood on a small table by the window, and said, "I expect you'd like a few moments to get yourself ready, wouldn't you?"

"Yes, please, sir."

"Well, you do that. And then off we go and we'll see how well you remember what the Comte de Servais said to you. Did you like him?"

"Oh, yes. He's a nice man. And when we had lunch there were all these birds flying around ... free. And they made messes, too—some on the table. He didn't seem to mind at all, did he, Dad?"

"No, son, he didn't. But I didn't fancy it much."

Peter said, "Although he's a Count he told me his real name was Alphonse Grubais, and he went to school in England and everyone called him All Grubby. I laughed at that and—"

"Peter." His father put out a hand and touched his shoulder. "Mr Rundell's a busy man. I think we should begin, don't you?"

"All right, Dad. Oh, Lord—was all that on the tape?"

Tampion laughed. "All there—for posterity. Don't let them hurry you, lad. Take your time."

Peter leaned forward in his chair and put his head in his hands. Grown-ups, he thought, were funny. Really funny.

Half the time you couldn't understand the whys and where-fores of them. Even Lady Diana. Why did she want him to do what she'd asked him? In a way it wasn't fair to Mr Rundell who'd paid money to his father. And not fair to his father to do something without warning him. But then ... well, it made no difference. Nobody but he knew what All Grubby had told him. He grinned behind his hands. Those birds. Once right on a roll the Count was holding and he had just broken the piece off and put it aside and winked at him. That was nice, too, the trip to France. And the Englishman fishing. And the station—the Gare Something—the Gare Saint-Laud.

He straightened up slowly and said, "I'm ready, sir."

Rundell took a piece of paper from his pocket and read slowly and distinctly, "Il était une fois un Grand Ours qui vivait en Orient et qui avait un tas d'enfants. Quand ceux-ci grandirent ils s'en allèrent gagner leur vie dans différents pays." He then stopped and put the paper back into his pocket.

Peter raised his head and looking at a picture on the far wall—it was one he had seen in other places of white-maned horses rising out of great, breaking sea rollers—began to speak.

"De temps en temps ils envoyaient à leur père des nouvelles sur les choses intéressantes qu'ils avaient vues et entendues...."

He spoke on, changing into English where the Count had, and then began to give names and addresses.

Tampion, sitting on the arm of a settee by the door, let his hand slide casually into his jacket pocket and fingered his automatic. Here came the names and, whether he was on the list or not, to be remembered by him. He couldn't match the boy for memory but a handful of names were no trouble par-ticularly as some of them he knew already. If his came ...

The boy spoke on, giving five names in all, and then stopped. After a moment or two of silence he took his eyes from the picture of the sea horses and said, "That's all, sir."

Rundell reached out, and switched off the tape recorder. "Marvellous," he said. "Absolutely marvellous. Now then, just to thank you for doing all this for me I've got you a present. But you're not to open it until you get back to this caravan where I understand you are staying. Promise?"

Peter smiled. "I promise, sir."

Rundell picked up a flat parcel wrapped in brown paper from the table with the recorder on it and handed it to Peter. Then he said to Peter's father, "Thank you both for coming. Most interesting. Most. What do you think, Teddy?"

Tampion grinned. "Think? I think it's bloody marvellous." And so it was—for there was no denying the relief in him to find that his name was not on the list. But he would have to do something about the ones which were. Rundell would lose no time getting them through to London. And—he could admit it to himself now—he was glad that he had not had to use the gun in his pocket. Go, dear boy, he thought, back into your own rosy little world. Enjoy it, old chap, while you have it. You'll never find another like it when you're grown up.

Peter stood up and said, "Is it all right if we go now? We're going to meet Judy. She's a friend of mine and came in with us. She's gone to see her aunt but she swore she wouldn't be long. You see, she didn't really want to go at all because this aunt of hers—"

"Peter." His father came and put an arm around him. "I don't think Mr Rundell wants to know about Judy."

"Oh, but I do. But perhaps some other time. Now, I'll see you down. Yes, and why not? I'll walk a little way with you. Where are you meeting her?"

"It's some church. Saint Andrew's, I think. Dad knows where it is."

"And so do I. I said my prayers there this morning. Come on then—and don't forget your parcel. What about you, Teddy?"

"No thanks. I'm full of ozone from this morning. I think I'll put my feet up for half-an-hour."

Tampion walked to the lift with them and saw them go down. Back in his room he took the automatic from his pocket and locked it in his suitcase. Thank God, he could admit now, that he hadn't been given cause to use it. Still, though he was not on the list, others were and they were fixed in his memory. They had to be warned before Rundell came back and got to work. He began to dial a London number, singing to himself—"*I've got a little list—I've got a little list. Of society offenders who might well be underground, And who never would be missed'.*" The sound of his own muted singing masked the turning of a pass key in his door.

Then, over the dialling tone of the telephone, a man's voice said, "Put it down, Mr Tampion, sir."

He turned to see two men who, though familiar to him, were no longer friendly towards him. Both held automatics. He put the receiver down, and then with a shrug of his shoulders said, "So I was on the list?"

"Yes, Mr Tampion, sir."

"But the boy dropped me off it?"

"Yes, Mr Tampion."

"Why?"

"I suppose you could say, Mr Tampion, for the love of a lady's blue eyes."

He shrugged his shoulders. "Well—I'm no wiser. But I'm soothed a little that it was done for love rather than money." He raised his arms, clasping his hands together, as they came and ran their hands over him for a gun, and said, "Perhaps I should have gone to jolly old church this morning."

Then as they finished their search and he lowered his hands, he let the right one pass over his mouth and with his tongue licked in the tablet which he had sprung from under the seal of his signet ring while they were together over his head. He had just time to say, "*Sic transit gloria* bloody *mundi*—what?" before the poison hit him and he toppled forward.

*   *   *   *

When they got to the church Mr Rundell shook hands with them both and then left. They had to wait some while for Judy. Then they went to the coach station and, as they sat waiting for it, Judy said, "What's in the parcel?"

"I dunno. It's a present from the man we went to see. I'm

174

not to open it until we get back to the caravan."

"Go on—don't be daft. Open it now."

"No, I promised. How was your aunt?"

"Just the same. All holy misery, and somebody pulled up all the wallflowers she'd planted in her front garden—so I helped her plant 'em again. She's mad about flowers. Outside and in. She's just had her parlour re-papered. You should see—all white and red roses. A real bugger it looks."

Standing a little from them Frank Courtney heard Peter's laugh and turned briefly to watch the two. They were as thick as thieves, he thought warmly. It was good to see them together and to hear their laughter ... a goodness of sight and sound that did something to him. The Rundell business was over. Thank God. They could go back to London and begin all over again. Tidy up the loose ends and put the recent past behind him. Rundell had got what he wanted and he could guess something of the importance of it all for his French had been good enough to get the broad message.

When they got back to Tavistock Lady Diana was waiting for them. As they drove back she said, "Just to finish off the day properly you're all to come up and have cold supper with me tonight. It's all right, Judy—I've fixed it with your mother for you to stay the night and I'll get you back early in the morning so that you'll be in time for school." She dropped Peter and his father at the caravan and drove on to Hightop Farm with Judy.

Once they were inside the caravan Courtney, grinning, said, "Well, now you can open your present."

Peter took off the wrapping and suddenly, pleased and excited, said, "How could he know? How could he?"

It was a pen-and-ink drawing, touched here and there with little washes of colour, of the great concourse at Paddington Station with the departure and arrival platforms in the background. In the foreground, as real as life, Peter thought, was Blackie Timms collecting his rubbish and over to one side was a woman in her kiosk who—with a little stretching of the imagination—seemed to look somewhat like May.

Frank Courtney smiled. "Mr Rundell's a clever man—and

he's got ways of knowing. You liked him, didn't you?"

"Oh, yes. Specially for this. But I really liked Mr Tampion more. He made me laugh that first time I met him. You know about '*Où est la plume de ma tante*' and why were French *tantes* always losing their blooming *plumes*." He was silent for a moment or two, looking at his picture and then keeping his eyes on it, he went on, "I don't have to do this memory thing any more, do I?"

"No. It's all finished."

"Good."

*   *   *   *

Winter-dry ash logs burned low in the fireplace. He sat taking brandy with his after-dinner coffee, watching the occasional spurts of blue-green flames.

She could see that he was relaxed. Anxiety and self-deceit were shrived from him and briefly she wondered if she should tell him the whole truth of what—through Lord Endsworth—she had done for Rundell—and then almost immediately decided against it. There was a time in life for speaking the truth and a time for keeping it hidden, especially when a man had moved through a period of self-discovery. Why load him with one more burden from the past?

She said, "You'll be going soon?"

"Yes, and you—" he paused and smiled, and it was a clear, understanding, slightly teasing smile, "—am I right in thinking you will be, too?"

She nodded. "I'm going to London to stay with old friends. Perhaps, I don't know, I may get a flat there and find something to do."

"Like what?"

"I wish I knew. But something will turn up." She smiled teasingly. "Would I be any good in a book shop?"

He laughed and shook his head. "None at all. Nobody would bother to look at the books."

*   *   *   *

176

In the kitchen Judy put a fresh cassette into the player and switched it on. The opening bars of a Strauss waltz filled the room.

Peter said, "That's not your kind of thing."

"Sometimes it is."

"Well, that's a new one."

"There's a lot of things you don't know about me. And about other people."

"For instance?"

"I think your father fancies her Ladyship."

Peter laughed. "Don't be daft. She's far too much above him."

"Think so? Lady Pillington over at Callington married her chauffeur last year. What was the present you got?"

"A drawing."

"What of?"

"Paddington Station."

"That's a funny sort of present."

"I like it."

She laughed and suddenly reached out and pulled his nose, saying, "You're a queer little bugger, aren't you?"

Also available by
VICTOR CANNING

THE FINGER OF SATURN
"Victor Canning has written a marvellously entertaining story of love and hate, of morality and evil, that I found impossible to abandon ... One of the best thrillers of the year."

Sunday Express

FIRECREST
"Hypnosis constitutes an interesting and original plot-factor, extremely well handled."

The Sunday Times

THE MASK OF MEMORY
"Very superior spy-story on two levels."   *Observer*

THE MELTING MAN
"A long, complicated, exciting and brightly written thriller by a master of the art with an international setting and a whole gallery of good characters."

Guardian

THE RAINBIRD PATTERN
"Wonderfully well-detailed and real plot concerning complex kidnap of topmost Establishment figure. The sheer imaginative weight holds you like a giant electro-magnet."

The Times

THE KINGSFORD MARK
"Fashioned with care and distinguished by sharp imagery and sense of excitement and menace."

Oxford Mail

THE DOOMSDAY CARRIER
"Enthralling from first to last."   *The Sunday Times*

BIRDCAGE
"Utterly absorbing."   *The Sunday Times*

178

THE SATAN SAMPLER
"Romantic, lush, heart-of-England thriller with slow-burning, suspenseful climax."

Guardian

FALL FROM GRACE
"Victor Canning must be one of our most prolific and reliable thriller writers."

Spectator

SMILER
A trilogy published in separate parts and now also obtainable in one volume comprising:

THE RUNAWAYS
"Beguiling little story of remand-home truant who meets another escapee on Salisbury Plain, a cheetah from Longleat expecting a happy event, and does the decent thing by the cubs when their mother is gored by an Ayrshire cow."

Observer

FLIGHT OF THE GREY GOOSE
"Smiler, who escaped from an approved school in *The Runaways,* is still on the run. . . . Mr Canning, who began his career as a writer about the countryside, has a nice touch and his pictures of scenery and animals are affectionately done."

The Times Literary Supplement

THE PAINTED TENT
"Excitement and thrills, with an appeal for most age groups and some incisive character drawing."

Methodist Recorder

An Arthurian trilogy published in three volumes:

THE CRIMSON CHALICE
". . . Fine bardic stuff that invests the old myths with the freshness of the morning and leaves one hungry for more."

Observer

8184